Orb

By

Emily Vaughn

Orb

Emily Vaughn

Published by Emily Vaughn, 2021.

ORB

First edition. January 28, 2021.

ISBN: 979-8223754428

Written by Emily Vaughn.

Table of Contents

For Uncle Dummy

Part One

The Project

It was about two o'clock in the afternoon when Patrick Night's small plane touched down in Mali. The tiny airstrip was hot and dry under the African sun. The makeshift airport consisted of one landing strip and a smattering of old dilapidated buildings that were used to house a couple of tiny aircraft such as that one that Night had only just been a passenger upon. The strip was just a long, wide swatch of earth that had been compacted and packed down and lined on the outside by rocks. The wind kicked up from the strip and swirled around him. The wind was sand in Africa. It stripped paint from cars, gathered in corners and under doors and in Bernard Alfonzelli's pockets as he moved to greet the Project's Technological Group Leader.

Bernard, Bernie as he was known by nearly all of his colleagues, had been sent to pick up the Tech GL at the tiny airstrip and drive him out to the dig site. Bernie was a personable man, and was used to meeting new people. Being very good at his job as well as a close personal friend of the Project Manager, the laborious task of driving people back and forth between the site and the airstrip had fallen to him. Generally he didn't mind, however, he found that he was a bit nervous this time. Being the Group Leader of the Dig Team for the Project, as well as a skilled linguist, Bernie was used to dealing with people. Night, on the other hand, dealt with computers and GPR and all things technological; all things inherently inhuman. Bernie's unease was based on the fact that he knew nothing of the technological and had no interest in it at all and that the long drive to the site would be a most boring one. Nevertheless, he was determined to at least attempt to make friends with this man, however geeky he may turn out to be.

Night was a tall, lanky fellow with short, straight, dark brown hair and glasses, quite the opposite of Bernie who was of below average height with a ruddy complexion and had put on a few too many pounds in recent years. Bernie did his best to smile pleasantly as he approached the man standing by the small plane. Secretly his smile was an anxious one, but he was sure he could fake it long enough to become pals with Night.

"Hallo" said Bernie in his usual cheerful way, but Night made no acknowledgement that he had heard him. Bernie cleared his throat and spoke again.

"Hallo...Patrick Night?" Again, there was no reply.

Night was, in effect, paralyzed. He had heard the calls of his colleague, but had been unable to utter so much as a syllable of a response. He had always been a nervous flyer, and the turbulent flight he just stepped off of was one of the worst he had ever been on.

"Are you Patrick Night?" Bernie said as he walked up next to the motionless man standing alone on the dusty airstrip. Night's expression was miles away. He stared into the distance unblinking and pale.

"I was...um...sent to..." Bernie began.

"Rick" said Night cutting Bernie off with startling abruptness.

"Call me Rick" he whispered then, as if the few words he spoke had been a catalyst for some unknown reaction in his body, Night bent over propping his hands on his knees and began to breathe heavily.

Raising one eyebrow at the man's strange behavior, Bernie then bent over so that his head was at the same level as Night's.

"Name's Bernie Alfonzelli, from Napoli, are... uh...are you okay?" he said kindly. Night merely rolled his eyes over to Bernie and back again to the dusty piece of land that lay between his feet. Bernie stood up straight again and sighed with dissatisfaction, but his resolve was absolute.

"So...How was your flight?" He asked somewhat sarcastically as it was obvious that Night was becoming increasingly sick, primarily, it seemed in the stomach region.

"I'm sorry, I just don't do well with travel" muttered Rick, trying to be sociable while simultaneously attempting to calm his churning stomach.

"Oh sure" said Bernie, smiling. "The flight from Sicily was hell, so, I understand completely". Night gave a slight nod but didn't speak, so Bernie continued to speak. Conversation was his tool for forging new friendships, and he was a man on a mission.

"Yeah, I really got tossed around up there, you know. Like being on a rollercoaster, you get shifted back and forth and up and down and you start to feel like a pinwheel inside you know; like your head is going round." He offered a sympathetic smile and added an encouraging "Right?"

Rick suddenly stood upright and Bernie had just enough time to secretly congratulate himself on a job well done. His freshly cracked smile didn't last long before turning to a grimace of disgust as Rick Night purged the contents of his stomach. Normally Bernie would have been more sympathetic, however the fact that the location of Night's lunch was now on his shoes meant that he was less than compassionate to his new friend's plight. Rick apologized profusely for his vomitous transgression. He was much more vocal now that he had relieved himself of the burden of his previous meal, but all of his newfound words were spent in the attempt to apologize to his colleague.

"Please, I'll buy you a new pair" Rick offered sympathetically, but Bernie, who was so talkative before, was silent. Bernie gazed a moment at his shoes, then at Night, who's expression was that of great woe.

Bernie then burst into a hearty laughter saying "Fuck it man, their just shoes".

Chapter 2

The ride out to the dig site was a long and bumpy ordeal which didn't serve to better Night's uneasy disposition. He was still feeling ill from his plane trip, and his airsickness had transformed into carsickness. Bernie was made to stop the vehicle several times during the drive, but unfortunately, he hadn't always stopped in time. By the time the pair arrived at the site, they were both a ghostly shade of white. The Jeep pulled to a halt in the parking area of the site which was little more than a group of vehicles disorderly placed on one side of the site. The billowing dust cleared to reveal the camp, which was an impressive spread of trailers and large tents. It was clear that the Project was well funded.

Samantha Byrne, PhD was the Project Manager of PhilTech's well funded endeavor. Sam, as she preferred to be called, was just exiting her large rectangular sleep tent when the Jeep arrived. She cocked half a smile at spotting the Jeep and set her heading to the parking lot. As she approached the two men, who were working at unloading the vehicle, she noticed that Bernie had for some reason removed his shoes and was now wearing a pair of flip flops that seemed to be a size or two smaller than his feet. This was particularly odd considering that the hot sun baked the sand to a scorching temperature well over a hundred degrees, not to mention that the red desert of Mali was known to house plenty of unfriendly creatures that lived beneath the sand. Sam, having known Bernie for many years now, knew of his particular aversion to scorpions and thus she concluded that the change in footwear was necessary, rather than voluntary.

She closed in on the position of her old friend and punched him casually in the arm. This was not an unusual greeting between the two, nor was teasing that, to an unwise observer, might seem cruel rather than playful.

"Nice shoes, going for a class clown award?" she mocked, but Bernie didn't respond in his usual manner.

"Oh, hallo Sam" he croaked as he continued to shift the bags and cases from the Jeep to the ground. His usual pleasant tone was missing and Sam immediately sensed that something was wrong. His chipper manner was something that she had come to count on in her friend of many years, but here, it was absent.

"Rough ride?" she inquired noticing that her friend was obviously not feeling well.

"Ugh...It was horrible" Bernie responded, swallowing loudly.

"Why don't you go sit down, get some water or something?" Sam said with genuine concern for the wellbeing of her friend and colleague. Bernie nodded and ambled off toward the water tent. Sam turned to find an equally pale Rick Night standing behind her holding a suitcase.

"You must be Patrick Night" she said extending her hand to him. He shuffled the suitcase to the ground then fumblingly shook her hand. She welcomed him professionally, though she was more concerned about Bernie at the moment. To be fair, she asked if he was well and then inquired about Bernie's condition.

"He... uh...or rather I...uh...I don't travel well" Night stammered. Then added "...and please call me Rick".

"I see" said Sam leaning back and glimpsing the mess inside the Jeep.

"Yeah, sorry about that" he offered sheepishly. Sam did not acknowledge his apology, but she hardly seemed angry. She turned back to Night and smiled brightly.

"Grab some stuff" she said "I'll show you around".

The two of them picked up the cases and bags of Rick's belongings and headed through the camp toward the sleep tent that was assigned to Patrick Night. On the way Sam pointed out the mess hall tent, the Showers, the Water tent and assorted other stations around the camp.

"That over there" she said, pointing at a trailer nearest to the large generator that ran the camp, "That's your work station, the Technology Lab".

"Great" he said in acknowledgement that he was pleased by what would be his office during his tour of duty at the dig.

"All of the equipment that you requested is already there and you will have the opportunity to set it up tomorrow" she said.

They continued to make their way through the large camp until they came upon the section of sleep tents. This section of camp was populated with large personal tents, each of which was rectangular measuring about eight by twelve feet at the base and six feet in height. It was rare to find such agreeable conditions in the field, or so Night had been told. He had never actually been on a field dig before, so all of this was very new to him. There was a certain amount of apprehension that he felt, but there was also a fair amount of excitement to accompany it.

"We certainly are well funded aren't we?" Rick commented upon seeing the huge sleep tent.

"Yeah well, Philpot Industries is banking a lot on this Project. That's why we are all here; we're all top notch in our fields." Sam said, raising both eyebrows briefly as if to say "lucky us".

"One thing I'm still not clear on though, why exactly *is* PhilTech Industries funding this Project, I mean...what's in it for them?" inquired Night.

"When they give us this much money, it's best not to ask too many questions," replied Sam, dismissively. "Here's your sleep tent". She dropped the bags in front of the large, canvas tent and placed her hands on her hips as if awaiting something.

"Thanks for your help," said Night, politely.

"Do you remember where the water tent is?" Sam said, referring to the large tent that housed several enormous tanks of fresh water that she had pointed out on their tour through camp. Night nodded to acknowledge that he did remember.

"I could really use a cold drink of water," he said.

"Well, the water is hardly cold, and I really more meant that you hook up the hose and rinse out the Jeep" she said curtly and gave a scrunched little smile.

"Welcome to the Project, Patrick Night" she said as she walked away.

"It's Rick" he said, but she either didn't hear, or didn't care.

Sam walked from the tent where she had left Night to unload his stuff alone, and headed toward the mess hall where she figured Bernie would be hanging out. The four sides of the huge tent were sectioned off, and each section could be tied up to create the desired amount of openness. Currently, all of the sides were lowered but one, which was the side facing the parking lot, meaning that from her present position, Sam was unable to see inside. She rounded the corner and peered in, but Bernie wasn't there. Perhaps he was in the kitchen trailer with Francois, she thought.

Francois was the Project's cook. He was a damn good one at that. Bernie had been stationed on several digs with Francois and the two men had become pals. Sam had only been on one previous job with him and she didn't know him very well, mostly due to the fact that she couldn't understand a word he said. Francois spoke only French and Swahili, usually at the same time. That compounded with his loud and fast, and generally forceful manner of speaking made it seem that he was constantly angry. One could say the same of Sam; that she seemed permanently pissed off, but in her case it was due to her aggressive and sarcastic nature. A left over from her Grad-School days. The unfortunate truth was that if you wanted to be a young, female Project Manager in her line of work, you had to be tough. That was Sam's opinion anyway, and she held to it. Only the smartest Archeologists made it to the field, and only the strongest of those actually survived there. This, perhaps, was why Sam considered herself superior in every way to most people.

She rounded the corner taking note that there were several power chords strewn across the gap between the mess hall and the kitchen. She would have to remember to tell Darrius, the camp coordinator, to tack those up lest someone trip and hurt themselves, she thought. She opened the door to the kitchen trailer and poked her head inside.

Bernie and Francois sat perched on stools opposite each other, laughing.

"Feeling better, I take it" she said with a smile.

"Hey! Sam, we were just talking about the drive from hell" Bernie said laughing "Come on in and sit down".

Francois said something that Sam couldn't understand and she looked to Bernie for a translation.

"He said that he is glad to see you but we must get out of his kitchen because he needs to begin preparing dinner" explained Bernie. Sam and Francois smiled briefly but kindly at each other then she and Bernie departed from the kitchen.

"Francois doesn't like me does he?" asked Sam once they were away from the trailer.

"He likes you, but you know how he is about too many people being in his kitchen" Bernie said. Sam shrugged, she didn't really know how he was at all, and she had never really devoted much time to getting to know him as communication was difficult. Francois could understand English just fine, but he either couldn't or wouldn't speak it.

"Did you get the geek all settled in?" Bernie asked, referring to Night. Sam nodded, ignoring his less than flattering nickname for their Tech man.

"I hope you told him to rinse out the Jeep" he said "I just don't know if I could handle the smell."

"I strongly suggested it" she replied. "So when are you going to tell me what's up with those ridiculous shoes." She laughed.

"I found them in the Jeep, I think they were Lishman's; she mentioned having lost a pair. Night vomited on my shoes at the airstrip" he said. Sam burst with laughter. "It seems he doesn't travel well" Bernie finished with a smirk. Sam contained her laughter for a moment and suggested that he go change his shoes. He shot her a look, but she only laughed harder.

"Just make sure the dig team is at the meeting tonight" she said, reminding him that it was his duty to translate her welcoming speech to those who didn't understand English.

"Are you nervous?" he asked.

"Me...never" she answered grinning.

With that, the two friends went their separate ways. Bernie went to his tent to change and Sam to her trailer to finalize her speech for the Welcoming that she was to deliver to the entire team just a short time from now. The truth was she felt some apprehension on the matter. She had given her share of addresses and speeches before, but never as the Project Manager. This was a huge deal to her and she always strove for perfection in her work. She was in uncharted territory as far as she was concerned, but there was nothing for it but to prepare.

Chapter 4

The mess hall was filled with the hum of conversation and chatter as the group of exactly one hundred and eighteen people filed in and found their seats. Sam and the other group leaders had seated themselves at a line of metal picnic tables that ran across the back side of the tent, perpendicular to the four other long rows. In the center of her line of tables, next to where Sam was seated, there was a short podium with a small microphone attached to it. The microphone was hooked up to six small speakers that were mounted onto the support poles in the center and rear sections of the large tent. Sam had seen then when she came in and the image of them had inspired that feeling of uneasiness to return. She shuttered briefly at the thought of her voice being amplified over the entire group. She had always liked her voice, but she really wasn't wild about the thought of so many people hearing it in surround sound.

Sam picked at her food, trying not to look out at the large crowd awaiting her speech. She was occupying her time by flicking green peas with her fork, attempting to shoot them through the center hole of the picnic table. Bernie, who had seated himself diagonally across from her, asked if she was feeling alright. She responded positively, but didn't look up, and Bernie was not convinced. He assumes that she was nervous about the speech after all. He could think of no other reason that she would be playing soccer with her food at a time like this. After years of being her friend, he had learned that she was proud, and therefore he did not press the matter.

Their conversation throughout the meal was sparse and bland, unlike the food. Francois had prepared barbequed lamb chops with mashed potatoes and green veggies. Francois was famous for his outstanding meals. Sam and Bernie had once been on a project with this guy from South Carolina who had said that 'Francois's cookin was s'good, make ya slap yer mamma.'

At the conclusion of the meal, Sam rose and placed herself in front of the short table podium. It wasn't much of a meeting place being sandy and hot, but somehow it felt so official as she repositioned the microphone. A single butterfly began to stir in her stomach as she looked out over the many faces of the Project team. She cleared her throat.

"Good evening" she said, deciding to begin simply. The sound of her voice was amplified and carried around the mess hall and the hundred and seventeen faces were suddenly staring back at her. Her butterfly was joined now by several more of its kin and they did cartwheels around her gut. She cleared her throat again and proceeded with her speech.

"My name is Doctor Samantha Byrne. I'd like to welcome all of you to the Project. I have worked with several of you before, but I am meeting most of you for the first time. I'm looking forward to working with all of you. And just to let you know...all the rumors you've heard about me are true." She paused briefly to await laughter, but very little came. She smiled and continued.

"Everyone should have received a packet in the mail. The packet includes, among other things, a map of camp, your personal duties and what's expected of you, a list of personnel, and tips for staying hydrated. There are several items that have changed, so pay attention. Firstly, the shower facilities are now located on the opposite end of the sleep tent area, so diagonal to the parking lot. Also, the outer guard perimeter now has a trailer equipped with an AC unit and a fridge." There was a howling response of praise from the guards. Sam smiled again and continued.

"Next, let's see, oh yes, the personnel changes. It seems Ira Shultz was added to the Tech group, and our new Tech Group Leader is Patrick Night, who's position was previously TBA on the list. In addition, the outer guard patrol was changed from sixteen to twenty-two people."

"Why so many?" asked a man seated at the table closest to Sam.

"I'll be happy to answer all questions at the conclusion of the speech." She answered, thinking how rude it was for him to interrupt her.

"Now, what I'd like to do is read off the names of some of our key personnel and if they wouldn't mind standing up briefly so everyone knows who they are." she paused and pulled a sheet of paper from her folder.

"Okay... Doctor Samantha Byrne, that's me, I'll be the Archeology GL...Group Leader.... as well as the Project Manager.

Doctor Margaret Lishman, Biology GL.

Doctor Maso Osami, Chemistry GL.

Patrick Night, Tech GL.

Bernie Alfonzelli, Dig Team GL, Dig Coordinator and Translator.

Jake Baxter, Security GL and Chief Guard.

Darrius Shifland is our Camp Coordinator and Group Leader of all Maintenance and Medical Personnel.

Amal Muhammad is our Local Relations Coordinator; he'll keep us informed of all local events and keep an eye on the weather for us.

And Francois... is our talented chef."

Sam didn't know Francois's last name. She had looked at Bernie briefly, hoping that he would mouth a name to her, but he was faced away from her while translating to the dig team. Sam smiled again and then thanked them for standing on command and concluded her speech by saying that all concerns could be presented to her by appointment or by stopping by the Arch. Lab between Two and Three O'clock in the afternoon.

"And now, if there are any questions..."

"Yeah, I have a question" said the impertinent man who had interrupted before. Sam acknowledged him. "Why on earth do we need so many guards?" he asked with a slight attitude.

"Well, just about every country on this continent is at war with every other country on this continent, so it's partially for our protection. In addition, our benefactors would like to ensure the secrecy and isolation of this project." She answered tersely. "Do we have any other questions?"

"Yeah," the man said again "Speaking of our benefactors, PhilTech Industries...why exactly are they funding this dig, I mean they deal mainly in technology, so why send a bunch of scientists out to the middle of Mali to dig up an ancient Temple? What do they have to gain by it?"

"I'm sorry what did you say your name was?" Sam asked suspiciously. The man was silent for a moment, clearly aware that he was being scrutinized. He rose quickly to his feet and bolted out the side of the tent.

"Someone, catch him" Sam shouted and several security guards rose from their seats to pursue. There was the sound of a car roaring out of the lot. A moment later the guards returned saying that they were unable to catch him before he drove away.

"Are you fucking kidding me?!" shouted Jake Baxter, Security Group Leader and head guard. "You call yourselves guards...can you at least tell me what type of vehicle it was?" he said, shaking his head.

"It was a black Hummer, boss" replied a guard named Alvarez. "No tags, no identifying markings of any kind, heavily tinted windows."

"Did it occur to any of you maggots to pursue in one of our Jeeps?" Baxter yelled.

"That's okay" said Sam quickly cutting him off "There's no need to bust their balls over one little mishap. I'm sure it's nothing."

Jake looked at her, surprised that she would let something like that go so easily. It was a clear breach in security. This man, this spy had driven right up to the camp and walked in like it was nothing. None of his team had noticed; nobody noticed, and now he just got away from them scot free. He thought it was very odd indeed that the PM wasn't the least bit angry about it.

Samantha concluded the Welcoming and wished everyone a good night. What had seemed to most as compassion was really only partially that. In truth, Sam was a little glad that the mysterious man had gotten away; after all he hadn't gotten anything useful out of it except for a few names, which meant very little with their level of security. Had they caught the spy, she would have had to explain the need for security as well as Philpot Industries' Involvement in the project. As it is, she was lucky that no one had asked why there would even be a spy on an archeological dig, but she could easily explain that away. She could play it off saying that he must have been a local news reporter or a brazen grave robber gathering information. They were lame excuses, but they were still more believable than the truth.

As Sam crossed the camp toward her trailer, she contemplated the events of the evening, and a crease began to form across her brow. She had always shown her stress on her forehead. Her mother was sure it would lead to wrinkles, but Sam was never able to keep her brow from forming little lines here and there whenever she was the least bit worried or stressed.

"You did good," said Bernie, startling her out of her state of deep thought. She smiled. "Weird though, about that guy, I mean...wanna talk about it?" he said holding up a bottle of Rum and smiling deviously.

"Hmm, tempting, but I have to get an early start tomorrow." She replied, smiling.

"Well I wasn't suggesting we pull an all-nighter or anything, just a drink or two." He said, feinting innocence.

"Ah...that old ploy," she said, squinting her eyes at him. "Last time we had 'just a drink or two'; we ended up staying up all night gambling."

"When?" said Bernie indignantly.

"Last year, at the symposium in Vegas," she said, raising her eyebrows.

"I don't remember...Oh...yeah I do. That was fun though" he said grinning.

Sam rolled her eyes and said "Good night Bernie".

He wished her a good night and left in the direction of the sleep tents. Sam swiped her key card to unlock the Archeology trailer, which held her office, and went inside. She sat down at her desk and put her files away. She kept them all in a locked drawer and wore the tiny key on a chain around her neck. Perhaps she was a bit paranoid, but in light of the evening's events, perhaps she was right on the mark. This locked drawer of hers also housed a bottle of Bushmill's Irish Whiskey, which Sam pulled out and placed on her desk. She sighed and opened the bottle and had a drink. She had many drinks that night while looking over the numerous personnel files and camp procedures. At midnight she rubbed her eyes and yawned. She put the files and the bottle back in her drawer, locked it, and exited the trailer. She walked through the clear, cool night, over the moon drenched sand and collapsed into her tent.

In her current state of exhaustion and intoxication she asked herself why she had turned down her good friend Bernie for a drink only to have one anyway, alone. For that matter, why had she not considered reveling with any of her colleagues? She chastised herself for being so exclusive, but then quickly dismissed the thought rationalizing that as the Project Manager it was her job to maintain a professional distance from her subordinates. Somewhere in the back of her mind was an annoying little whiskey soaked thought that refused to dissipate. Was she really so quick to dismiss so many people, so many colleagues, as potential friends. Did she have so many friends that she needed no more? These thoughts floated around her brain like ghosts as she drifted off to an uneasy sleep.

The fact was that Samantha Byrne had never had many friends. Apart from Bernie, a few other colleagues, and an old college professor of hers, she was quite a solo person most of the time. She never saw herself as lonely though. Sam was very close to her parents, and her cat, Mouser. Her work was her constant companion, and mostly that suited her. Occasionally, though, she did wonder why she hadn't been on a date in so long. More to the point, she wondered why she insisted upon her own solitude, if she only resented it later.

Perhaps her mother said it best. Mrs. Byrne would frequently look at her daughter and say "Samantha, dear, why is such a lovely young lady as yourself so alone? Why don't you find yourself a nice young man to grow old with?" Sam was lovely, tall and trim with well placed curves and long straight brown hair. Men certainly found her very attractive. Her youth and beauty caused more than a little attention from the opposite sex. To Sam, it was tiresome to be hit on so frequently. For this reason, she had learned to avoid public bars and coffee shops. But her seclusion only served to increase her solitude and work-a-holism.

Perhaps this was why she and Bernie got along so well. He was never anything but a friend to her. Not once in their years together had he ever made so much as a pass at her. In her arrogance, Samantha suspected that he might be homosexual though he didn't act like the stereotype. She could think of no other reason why he had never looked upon her with lustful eyes. In fact, Bernie was not gay at all. It was as simple an explanation as could be, though Sam never understood. Bernie thought of her as a sister; a pal, and nothing more. In turn, she thought of him as her closest friend and confidant, but was hubris enough to question his sexuality. Sam's arrogance was not altogether unwarranted as she was undoubtedly more beautiful and more intelligent than most, but it was her biggest flaw. Still, following suit, she was scarcely aware of her own egotism, and hardly thought it was a problem.

The chaos and hustle of the following day rang noisily in Sam's head. She maintained her professionalism quite well throughout the day despite her splitting headache. By the time lunch rolled around, she was feeling her old self again. Her faith in herself as a Project Manager was at its peak again, after being slightly shaken the previous night. She wouldn't admit that her confidence was lowered; only that it was heightened now. She had, for the entirety of the morning, helped get things set up, answered questions and generally managed the group. This pleased her, and she felt a great sense of worth. By two-thirty or so, she was even more pleased to find that most of the teams were completely set up with the exception of a few minor issues that she had already delegated to the appropriate people. With everything ready for the next day, which was set as the day to begin the actual digging process, she decided to sneak a short nap in before her GL meeting at five.

Chapter 5

S he opened her eyes groggily and as they cleared of their sleepy fog, they fell upon her watch that was hanging next to her bed. To her surprise it read four forty-five. "Shit" she said aloud as she jumped to her feet. She pulled her tangled hair onto a sloppy ponytail and hot-footed it to her trailer to pick up her files. She had hoped to shower before her meeting, but that was out of the question now. She only hoped that she didn't smell as a result of the day's heat and hard work.

Upon arriving at the Archeology Lab, she realized, painfully, that her keycard and desk key were still in her tent hanging up with her watch. Incidentally, that meant that she had left her tent unlocked as well. All of the sleep tents had loops, inside and out, attached to the zippers that served to open and close the door to the tent. Everyone was issued a padlock that could be placed through the loops and thusly, the tent would be locked. Of course, if someone really wanted to get in, they could have just cut through the side of the canvass, but the point was more that no one would be tempted to just see themselves inside at their leisure. If nothing else, the locks provided a certain sense of security that eased the mind in an unfamiliar place. Sam's mind was not at ease though as she hurried through the camp to her tent. She grabbed her things and locked her tent, then rushed back to the trailer to recover her files. Having done so, she set at a run to the mess hall, which was the location that had been set for the daily five o'clock GL meetings.

As she sprinted through the camp, she couldn't help but think of how impatiently her crew must be awaiting her arrival. They were no doubt wondering where she could possibly be. She wondered if they could ever really respect a leader who couldn't even show up on time for their very first meeting. As her pace quickened and her mind struggled to focus, she failed to notice where she was going. She tripped over the power chords that she had noticed the previous day, and as she fell, the painful irony on the situation set in. She hit the ground with a thud, her chest and arms leading. The wind was knocked out of her and she had inadvertently released a vocalization of her pain in the form of a sharp cry. Her papers and files surrounded her on the sandy ground.

The fact that she had fallen was fine, the thick oilcloth sides of the mess hall tent were down so the GLs inside hadn't seen her little mishap. Someone had seen her, though. It was that fact that truly caused her to be bruised more so than the fall itself. From her dusty vantage point she was aware of a pair of legs in front of her, though she did not yet know to whom they belonged.

"Let me help you" said a voice as he helped her from the ground. The voice and the legs belonged to Night, and Sam swallowed her embarrassment as best she could.

"Thank you Mister Night" she said coldly and dusted herself off.

"Sure, sure" he said "Let's pick up those papers before they blow away". He bent forward and began to collect the scattered pages from the red sand.

"Thank you, that won't be necessary," she said, snatching the pages from his hands.

"I was only trying to help," he said, sensing her hostility, "It looked like a nasty trip".

"Not as nasty as yours Mister Night, at least I didn't vomit after my trip" she replied, infuriated. Then she collected up the last of her files from the dirt and disappeared behind the tarp followed shortly thereafter by Night.

"Ah, you've found her" said Margaret Lishman in her thick British accent. She sat away from the rest of the group.

"Sorry I'm late, I had a minor setback" Sam said, apologetically.

"We were beginning to get worried," teased Bernie.

"Well I'm here now, so let's get this meeting underway. Lishman, isn't it, why have you ostracized yourself from the rest of the group?"

Sam asked referring to the fact that the woman sat alone several tables away from the others.

"It's the smoke from her cigarette, it has always bothered me" answered Maso Osami, Chemistry GL.

"I'll put it out already," Lishman said, rolling her eyes and putting out her cigarette. She joined the others at the picnic table where they sat huddled in a small group.

"Very well, now that that's solved, shall we begin?" Sam's tone was more annoyed than she had wanted it to be, but she attempted to compensate for her bad mood as they spoke. They discussed a variety of subjects ranging from, but not limited to, chain of command, communication, water and sewer service, and emergency procedure. Doctor Maso Osami found fault with nearly everything and Sam's limited patience was wearing thin. When she explained that the drinking water tanks were filled every other day, he asked what they would do if they ran out of water. Sam had assured him that it wasn't a concern as the tanks were far and above what they needed for one hundred and eighteen people for two days. When she explained that the Toilet facilities were maintained every other day, he asked if he could switch tents with someone as he was very close to them and was concerned about the smell and possible spillage. Sam again assured him that his concerns were unwarranted.

"They aren't your every day, run of the mill port-a-johns. They are the best that money can buy. They even have hand washing stations with running water inside each one." Sam said, attempting to clarify.

"Well I should hope so" was his response.

Sam left it alone and continued her monologue on emergency procedure.

"We have three fully trained Field Paramedics on staff here in the camp each of them has a different eight hour shift so there's always one available and two on call." She was attempting to present it in a way that would silence Osami, but he still managed to find something to complain about.

"Medics! You mean to tell me that we don't have a real Medical Doctor here at all!" cried Osami, quite alarmed.

"The Field Medics are perfectly capable of treating anything from a hangnail to a broken leg, Dr. Osami, and it is my hope that we won't need them at all." Sam said allowing her irritation to show through.

"Still...what if something terrible were to happen, you can't tell me we are just supposed to cross our fingers and hope for the best." He argued.

"No Doctor, in a medical emergency situation, we will be able to contact an emergency medical evacuation helicopter that will quickly retrieve the injured and get them to safety."

"But..." he protested, but Sam cut him off before he could whine anymore.

"That will conclude our discussion of emergency procedure" she said the words clearly and slowly and stared him in the eye as she spoke. It got her point across. Osami silenced himself after that.

"Now, if there are no more questions..." she said, pausing to allow anyone to speak.

"Then this meeting is adjourned" and with that she scooped up her scrambled stack of papers and set them aside. It was now six fifteen, time for dinner. Francois had been floating in and out throughout their meeting and the tables on each of the long sides of the rectangular mess hall were now filled with food. People were beginning to file into the tent in anticipation of whatever goodies tonight's dinner buffet might hold.

Bernie came to sit next to Sam who was clutching her head in frustration. He placed his hand on her shoulder in a friendly gesture.

"Do you want me to get you a plate of food?" he asked.

"Thanks" she said "Do I look as hungry as I feel?"

"Well, on that I couldn't say, I just thought that you might like to sit for a while, you look like you've had a hard day, what with those bloody elbows and all." Bernie raised his bushy eyebrows as he walked off toward the buffet line. Sam glanced at her skinned elbows before placing her head back into her hand and giving a heavy sigh.

"They're never going to take me seriously are they?" she said once he returned with two plated of food. Bernie chuckled.

"I think your problem isn't that they don't take you seriously, but that you take yourself far too seriously." He chuckled again.

They two sat and chatted over their dinner. Sam was beginning to feel better, until Bernie happened to mention how quiet some of the GLs had been at the meeting.

"Osami certainly had plenty to day" Sam whispered to Bernie, as the subject of their conversation was seated close by.

"No kidding, I've never heard someone complain so much in one sitting." Bernie whispered back and they both laughed.

"You don't think I was too hard on him do you" She asked sincerely.

"No, he was annoying everyone, he was being ridiculous really" answered Bernie.

"I noticed Baxter and Darrius didn't have anything to say either." Sam said.

"No, as well they shouldn't this early in the game, if they had anything to report I should have been very nervous" said Bernie laughing a little. "The geek didn't speak either".

"You mean Night?" She said pushing her food around on her plate a little. Bernie was fluent in many languages, and body language was not excluded.

"What did you say to him?" he asked. He knew her well and knew that she had a tendency to say hurtful things to people, though she always felt awful about them later. Sam relayed the story of her nap and the escapade of her keys and her unfortunate luck of falling down right in front of the geeky Tech GL. Then she sheepishly confessed to being quite rude to Patrick Night, though she thought her one-liner about the trip was quite clever. Bernie could see she felt badly about it. He knew that if he suggested that Sam apologize to Night, that she wouldn't, out of pride, but that if he said nothing, that it would eat her up inside until she would apologize out of guilt. Thus, Bernie said nothing further on the subject.

Chapter 6

Rick sat quiet and alone in the Tech Lab. He could only hear the low hum of the computers which suited him just fine. It was a noise that soothed him; comforted him. It seemed he was always alone with his computers and his thoughts. He rarely participated in group work, but he was one of the best in his field and was therefore asked to join the Project as Technological Group Leader. He had declined at first, but ultimately accepted after being offered a large incentive. As he sat alone in the trailer contemplating whether or not the money was compensation enough for the travel and the daily insults.

He was painfully aware that he didn't fit in. Everyone had their little cliques around here. It was like high school all over again. Bernie was the cool dude that everyone seemed to know and like. Lishman and Osami knew each other from Oxford and, though they bickered, they were good friends. Baxter was the archetype jock, handsome and muscular. Darrius was the class president, always informed of everything that was going on. Samantha, well, Sam was every cheerleader, every pretty girl who he had ever spoken to. Beautiful and cruel, she was smart and quick witted at that. Such a gorgeous woman and yet to look into her beautiful eyes was to be stung by her venomous tongue. Her words were every bit as sharp at her wit. Rick felt like such a toad next to her. What a shame that her personality couldn't match her lovely exterior.

Rick sighed and decided that he would just have to focus on the Project and not worry about the politics of it all. He started fidgeting with one of the GPR scanners, attempting to adjust the picture readout. He wasn't pleased with the quality of the image so he kept messing with it until finally the knob had enough and came right off in his hand.

He held the tiny plastic knob in his hand and shook his head. There was an abrupt knock on the door which made Rick jump suddenly and the thing went flying out of his hand and under the desk.

"Just a minute" he shouted as he got on his hands and knees and crawled under the desk to find the knob.

"Oh!" exclaimed Sam as she entered the room to find Night on all fours with his head under a table. She giggled a little at the sight. Her entrance was not at all expected and had again jumped this time hitting his head on the underside of the table.

"I'm so sorry, I didn't mean to startle you" said Sam, still laughing a little.

Rick, having retrieved the knob to the scanner, shuffled himself out from under the desk and got to his feet. He rubbed his head.

"Is there something I can do for you?" he said, slightly annoyed.

"No...well yes...I mean...is this a bad time?" she stammered.

"Well that depends" he replied coldly "have you come to discuss the project or did you just want to see if I had thrown-up again after the walk from the mess hall to here?"

She giggled a little at the thought saying "well it is quite a trek". Her genuine smile made her seem even prettier and Rick couldn't stay annoyed at seeing it. He sat down in his chair more at ease than before.

"What did you need" he asked more pleasantly than before.

"Just to...um...apologize" Sam said nervously.

"Apologize?" said Rick, surprised.

"For earlier" she said "I behaved..."

"Like a bitch" he offered an ending to her sentence, smiling dryly.

"Well...yeah, so look I'm sorry I was rude and...Sorry" she fumbled her words, but gave a decisive nod at the end as though that was exactly what she meant to say.

"That wasn't much of an apology" he said "but I accept".

"You know, it isn't easy for me to...I've worked very hard to get here...sometimes I just...people need to take me seriously. They need to know I'm in charge." Samantha was so mad that she couldn't finish her own sentences.

"Let me see if I understand you correctly..." he began "You make fun of people so that they'll respect you?" He shot her a look that seemed to say, I know you're not that stupid. Sam was silent.

"It seems to me that you are in charge...People tend to respect a leader who is compassionate more than one who is..."

"A bitch" Sam finished for him.

Night nodded and they were both quiet for a moment before Sam spoke again, this time in hushed tones.

"I'm sorry; I was very insensitive this afternoon. I was embarrassed and I guess I needed to embarrass you to feel better about my own predicament. It was wrong of me." she paused for a long time before adding "see you in the morning Patrick Night" and then she was gone as suddenly as she had arrived. Night was stunned. She had clearly put a lot of effort into her apology, although it was still pretty shabby. She still called him Patrick, but this time he was willing to let it go. Before turning his thoughts back to the scanner and the broken knob in his hand, a curious notion crept into his mind. Perhaps Samantha Byrne was human after all.

Chapter 7

The next morning was dark. Four thirty was marked by full shower stalls and lines for the coffee in the mess hall. Breakfast wouldn't be served until seven and lunch at eleven thirty followed by a mid-day break from the heat and the work. Then, back to work at two thirty until the GL meeting at five and dinner at six thirty. The day would be long and full for everyone. This day marked the first of many to come. Eventually it would become routine, but Sam expected that these first few would be the most difficult.

Jake Baxter walked briskly and purposefully through the busy camp from the mess hall. His destination was the set on the Archeology Trailer, which was becoming known as the Dry Lab as all of the specimens examined here would be lifeless objects. By comparison, the Biology Lab was called the Wet Lab as all of their specimens would be biological in nature; once living, though probably no longer so if they were to be examined there.

Jake didn't have much use for these scientist types, however he made no complaint about meeting with the beautiful and buxom Samantha Byrne. He was intent on discussing last night's patrol with the lovely Project Manager. As he rounded the side of the Wet Lab he was bumped into by someone he was not expecting to see; Doctor Margaret Lishman.

"Ooh, pardon me" she said pleasantly.

He only nodded politely to her, and then went on about his way. When he arrived at the Dry Lab, however, Byrne wasn't there. Her team was there, though, and they informed him that Sam was still at the showers but would be along shortly. He thanked the five of them and left. For a moment he thought about what it would be like to see Samantha in the shower. He smiled at this mental image as he walked to the guard tent on the edge of the dig site.

Upon arriving he was met by several of his day shift guards. They inquired about his meeting with the PM.

"She's in the shower" he replied. His guards hooted playfully.

"Yeah, when I see her next I'm going to suggest that we hold all of our meetings in there" he laughed.

"Yeah, she's hot, but I gotta girl at home who's even hotter," said Alvarez.

"Bullshit, you ain't got no babe back home" teased Chet Mahoney.

"You wanna see a picture, asshole?" retorted Alvarez digging for his wallet. He produced a picture of a busty brunette with plump lips and mocha skin. "This is Angela" he said with a grin.

"Whoa! What a fox" said Mahoney.

"Yeah, I bet she fucks like a minx too, right?" said Baxter in disbelief.

"You know it man" answered Alvarez.

"Yeah right...I bet this is a picture of your sister" said Baxter, laughing.

"You wanted to see me?" Sam said loudly busting into the conversation. Jake turned to find her standing with her hands on her hips. He was silent for a second as he tried to figure out how long she might have been standing there.

"Did you want to see me?" she said again.

"Lady, you have no idea!" Alvarez said, laughing.

"Alvarez!" shouted Baxter "Go get me some coffee".

"But boss..." Alvarez began, motioning to the fresh cup of coffee that Jake was holding.

"Just go...NOW!" he shouted with a tone that clearly implied 'or I put my foot up your ass' and so Alvarez departed.

Sam began to tap her foot impatiently, hands still on her hips.

"Sorry...Perhaps we should speak in your office" said Baxter.

"Fine" she said brusquely, turning and walking toward her office in the Dry Lab. As he followed, Jake made no attempt to veil the fact that he was enjoying the motion of her body as she walked. Once in her office Sam made a point of putting a sweater on over her tank top. She was very familiar with the type of leer that Baxter was giving her.

"I'll let you read it later" he said plopping a report on her desk "but here are the highlights". He sat down in a chair on the opposite side of the desk from her.

"May I sit?" he said.

"Go ahead," she said, raising her eyebrows.

"So, round about midnight there was a vehicle that circled camp a few times; a black Hummer." He said.

"You're sure it wasn't one of our Jeeps" she said.

"Heh" was his only response.

"It was spotted by the Outer Patrol?" she asked referring to a group of twenty-two guards that formed a perimeter far out from the actual camp and dig site.

"Actually, it was spotted from the guard post inside the camp" he said.

"How did that happen?" Sam was considerably more concerned now.

"They were running without headlights. There's a lot of desert out there and they just slipped in." he said shrugging.

"Do you suspect grave robbers?" Sam asked, actually hoping he would say yes.

"Grave robbers...not likely; I think it may have been our friend from the welcome meeting" he said.

"Well I suspect that he was a grave robber, just scoping us out, gathering information" she said. Jake was silent. He knew that there was no way she could be that stupid, so he assumed that he was being hassled. Jake did not like to be hassled.

"Grave robbers" he said again "...yeah..."

"Do you have another theory, Baxter?" Sam asked, challenging him.

"What the hell are you hiding from everyone? What the fuck is this dig really about" he shouted.

"I don't appreciate being yelled at," said Sam coolly.

"Yeah, well I don't appreciate being kept in the dark" he said shortly.

With that Sam stood up and said "Thank you for your report Mr. Baxter, I'll review it carefully. Until we know more, please proceed under the assumption that we are dealing with grave robbers." She crossed the room and opened the door; a professional and polite way of kicking him out of her office. He grunted indignantly as he exited past her into the main room of the Dry Lab trailer. He nodded to the two Grad-students then exited the trailer. He was then bumped into again by Lishman.

"Ooh, pardon me" she said as before, smiling. Jake huffed, annoyed and angered, then disappeared around the corner of the lab.

Chapter 8

Margaret Lishman was a skilled Biological and Cultural Anthropologist by vocation, and a knowledgeable zoologist by avocation. Celebrated and decorated over many years, she was the top in her field and what she lacked in looks, she more than made up for in intellect. Short and dumpy with unkempt hair and thick glasses, Lishman's most attractive feature was her mind. Tested as a child, her Intelligence Quotient was off the charts at one hundred and eighty one. This meant that she was given every academic advantage, allowing her to graduate from University at the tender age of sixteen. She went on to Graduate School at Oxford and got her first PhD at twenty, by twenty-three she had her second. She took a year off to backpack across Europe before returning to Oxford for a third time, this time as a Professor. It was this time around that she had the pleasure of getting to know Maso Osami, who was a student at the time. By twenty-six she was the head of the Anthropology Department at Oxford. Four years later at thirty years old she was offered a job as curator of the Museum of Cairo. The pay was about the same, but she jumped at the occasion. She had always had a certain appreciation for Egyptology, and saw it as a most unique opportunity to further her understanding of the subject. As it turned out, she didn't much like living in Egypt, so she returned to merry old England at thirty two. She went back to teaching, this time at a small university in Manchester, where she has lived happily for seven years. Now at the age of forty, she is on a most exciting dig in Mali, and, more specifically, she is on her way to see Doctor Samantha Byrne.

After bumping into Jake Baxter, she resumed her course to the Dry Lab. She swiped her key card, but the door didn't open. She tried again and received the same blinking red light as a response. All of her intelligence and yet she was unable to open a door. Finally she resorted to knocking. Karissa Pittman, Grad-Student and top of her class at UT, opened the door a few seconds later.

"Good morning Miss Lishman" she said cheerfully as Margaret came inside.

"Oh, I simply can't imagine what could possibly be wrong with my key card" she said, frustrated.

"Oh, but Miss Lishman, that's not your keycard, that's a credit card" Karissa said, trying not to laugh.

"Oooh, so it is, I see now. Well then where the devil is my key card" she said.

"Try your wallet" said Brad Harris, the other Grad-Student.

"Oh yes, that's a good idea, thank you" she said smiling "is Samantha around?"

"She's in her office" said Karissa and pointed at the open door at one end of the trailer.

Chapter 9

Margaret entered the office and greeted Sam warmly. The two discussed some issues that the Wet Lab was experiencing.

"The cooling unit seems to be leaking" Margaret explained "it's dripping all over the carpet, and I'm concerned that it's going to mildew and contaminate the environment of the lab."

"I'll let Darrius know, he'll get a maintenance guy to look at it immediately" Sam responded.

"Sam, are you alright, you seem tense" Margaret asked out of concern.

"I'm fine, I just had a most unfortunate meeting with Jake Baxter" she said.

"Ooh, how could anything involving that man be unpleasant" giggled Margaret.

"I don't think I know what you mean," said Sam, a little disgusted.

"I've bumped into him twice today. It was like running into a brick wall, Oh I love men with muscles!" Margaret's face blushed girlishly. Sam laughed at her school girl attitude. Margaret sighed heavily and said "you know he smells like old spice".

Sam was truly repulsed by the man, but she enjoyed seeing Margaret get hot and bothered.

"C'mon let's go out to the dig site, we can walk past the Guard House on the way and you can blow kisses to him." The two ladies giggled and departed the lab.

They crossed the sandy, open gap that separated the camp from the dig and made their way past the guard tent. Margaret smiled and waved playfully at Baxter, who grimaced in disgust in return. He was into pretty girls, not brainy women, and certainly not thick glasses and, undoubtedly, granny panties.

Chapter 10

The two met up with the others at the dig site. Sam spoke to Darrius about the problem with the AC unit in the Dry Lab and so he toddled off over the smooth red sand back to camp.

Sam inquired as to how everything was going with the dig. The site was mostly sand at this point, but one section of the dig was home to what the team referred to as the 'good stuff'. There was a large portion of some ancient structure poking its head out of the sand. The stone was barely uncovered, but still it was amazing to see. The preliminary tests had dated the ancient stone to be from roughly 3600 BC. Whatever this temple was, it predated Mesopotamian cities by a hundred years, the birth of ancient Egyptian civilization by about five hundred years, and the Early Minoan Era of Ancient Greece by about six hundred years. This site was ancient. It wasn't even clear what civilization had built it. It was mostly this fact that had brought them all here. It was certainly a significant find, and that was just the tip of the iceberg. Such a small portion had yet been uncovered. There was much work to do.

"This is cool," said Chris Martin from Australia, who was on Night's staff. Chris was responsible for executing the proper use of all technological equipment in the field. In Bernie's words, he's the geek who actually goes outside, and he gets to hold the expensive stuff. Chris was showing Sam some kind of high-tech piece of equipment.

"It looks like a big, fancy metal detector," She said.

"Nah, it's much cooler than that," he said with a grin. "This baby is a brand new GPR hand held unit with a modified amplification unit attached. I built her, and now we get to see her in action." He hooted with laughter, apparently thrilled. Sam thought he sounded like the geek version of the Crocodile Hunter, only instead of stalking wildlife, Martin was excited by technology.

"What the hell did you just say?" asked Bernie.

"GPR...Ground Penetrating Radar" said Chris.

"It's how we get to see under the sand before digging" added Night, who was just arriving.

"Are we all set in the lab?" asked Chris

"Check" replied Night.

"Okay...watch this!" Chris said excitedly. He flipped a switch on the handle of the device and began to wave it over the sand around the location of the stone.

"Whoa! Are you getting this? This baby's huge" exclaimed Chris with his eyes fixed on the tiny screen of the handheld GPR scanner.

"Chan and Shultz are in the lab now, they're receiving you just fine" replied Night.

"Patrick, could we go to the lab and take a look?" asked Margaret.

"Yeah, sure" said Night, shrugging. "Chris, you keep at it, see if you can at least get us a perimeter" he said to his wide eyed colleague. "Right this way and please call me Rick". Night motioned to signal an unspoken 'follow me'. Margaret, Sam, and Pete Thatcher, Archeologist, followed him to the Tech Lab. Bernie opted to stay behind to coordinate the diggers who were slaving away under the already hot morning sun; working hard to clear away as much of the surrounding sand as possible. Pete had left the other Archeologist, Mike Morrison, in charge of the two Grad-Students who were brushing sand from the exposed section of the structure with care and precision.

Arriving at the Tech trailer, Night swiped his key card and opened the door for the others. The cool air from inside washed over them. They could feel their skin reacting to the sudden and extreme change in temperature. Sighs of respite and relief were uttered by all.

"Rick, take a look man this is incredible" said Cris Chan, technological expert that Night has brought on as support on the Project.

"Wow" exclaimed Rick as he leaned onto the desk next to Chan's computer. Margaret, Pete and Sam shrugged signaling that they had no clue as to what they were really seeing.

"So where's the head?" Sam said sarcastically. She received a chuckle from the group due to the resemblance of the image on the screen to a prenatal sonogram.

"Actually, that's sonar, what you are looking at here is radar," said Ira Shultz dryly.

"Oh I see, thank you for clarifying" Sam replied brusquely.

"You're welcome" Shultz said smiling, clearly missing her sarcastic tone.

"What you're looking at here..." said Rick, pointing at the screen "...these are solid bits"

"Sorry, solid bits?" asked Margaret, who didn't seem able to see any of what they were looking at and kept leaning in closer and closer to the screen.

"Anything more dense than sand" said Rick, clarifying "and with Chris' modifications, we should be able to get a rough idea of the layout inside the structure".

"You mean we'll have a map of the temple before we even get inside?" said Pete.

"Sure, and if we set the GPR to the density of the stone, we might even be able to see other stuff too, like bronze or gold artifacts inside the structure. As for a map, we should have something of a rough 3D image in a couple of days" Night said proudly.

"Excellent work guys" Sam said in a rare display of congratulations.

The group then disbanded and returned to their respective tasks. Pete to the dig site, Chan and Shultz remained in the Tech Lab and Margaret headed for her lab to check the status of the cooling unit. Sam had decided that it was time to get some water and so she headed in the direction of the water tent. She was joined by Rick, who had the same desire as she for refreshment.

They walked together discussing further the virtual imaging and the process of mapping of the structure.

"Seems like you've got a good team" said Sam referring to his support staff.

"Not bad for a group of geeks, huh" he said laughing.

"You all seem to work well together, except for maybe Shultz. He seems a bit...vanilla if you catch my meaning" said Sam.

"Ugh, he has no sense of humor at all" said Rick, agreeing with Sam's flavorful description of his colleague.

"Then why did you choose him?" asked Sam. Rick paused a moment.

"He wasn't my choice, PhilTech assigned him. I only chose Chris and Cris, Chris Martin and Chan, as we call the other one. I didn't even know Shultz was on my team until you announced him the other night." Night seemed surprised that Sam didn't know that, being the PM and all.

"I see...I'll have to ask Steve about that next time I talk to him." She said, referring to Steve Philpot, CEO and Founder of PhilTech Industries. "Oh, that reminds me, is that video satellite thing set up yet? I'm supposed to report to him regularly."

"The satellite phone is good to go, and it's already set up with the video interface. Just let me know when you need to use it, it's a bit temperamental." He handed a cup of water to Sam and grabbed one for himself.

'Thanks Patrick, ' she said.

Night shook his head. "Rick, my name is Rick".

"Sorry, I just can't seem to remember. What's wrong with Patrick anyway?" she said.

"I just really hate being called Patrick. Everyone calls me Rick" he answered.

"I promise I will try to remember," Sam said, finishing her water. Then she took her leave of the water tent and went to reapply some sunscreen. Rick returned to his lab with a slightly better opinion of Samantha Byrne than he had before. Sam's opinion of him had not much changed though. She still saw him as a geek, but a competent one. Sam generally thought of most people as completely useless. Of course there were those who were somewhat capable, but generally speaking, there were very few she awarded the title of competent. In this way, one might say that she held Rick in high regard. In her mind, though, all were inferior to her. Despite her arrogance, she felt a slight respect for him, but would never admit to as much.

Chapter 11

She returned to the dig site with a bottle of SPF 50 that she had retrieved from her tent. She passed it around to the grateful group of fair skinned scientists. The diggers mostly wore robes to protect their skin from the sun. The majority of the diggers were locals and were more accustomed to the burning sun, but the rest of them had to take serious precautions. Chris Martin, was still wandering around, waving his device slowly back and forth over the sand. Being from Australia, one might assume that he was used to getting sun, but in fact, he had been stationed on a project in Siberia for the better part of a year before coming out to Mali. He was starting to crisp into a frightening shade of vermillion, so Sam left her crowd of Archeologists to take the sunscreen lotion to him. She approached him saying some generic greeting, but he didn't hear her. As she got closer, she realized that he was wearing a pair of headphones. She rolled her eyes and tapped him on the shoulder. He jumped in surprise and yanked the headphones off his head.

"God, you scared the hell out of me" he cried.

"Here, you should put some of this on; you're beginning to resemble a cooked lobster." She handed him the sunscreen. "What are you listening to anyway?" she asked.

"Metallica" he said, throwing up a 'rock on' sign with his fingers and head banging for effect. Sam chuckled at his display. She stood with him for a moment while he applied the sunscreen, then, taking the bottle back with her; she headed back toward her crew. On her way, she overheard a clip from a conversation between two support staff members. What they seemed to be discussing was troublesome to Sam. They were talking about the Project and one of them commented on the strangeness of their being there on PhilTech's dime. They conversed a moment on the subject saying things like "what interest could PhilTech possibly have in an ancient temple?" and "I feel like our superiors are lying to us". Sam was becoming more concerned. Too many people were asking questions that she couldn't answer. She was worried that it may lead to discontent amongst the group. It was her job to manage everyone on location; to keep them happy, and she wasn't pleased with the thought of failing in that capacity. This was her first command; her first time as a fully fledged Project Manager, and she was determined that she would make it a success.

Lunch rolled around and she listened out for similar conversations to the one that she had overheard before. She wanted to gather information, to know what was on her crew's mind. Perhaps it was a bit paranoid, but Sam would rather be paranoid about nothing than oblivious to a real threat. To her, discontent about the Project was very much a hazard, a dark shadow that floated around and threatened to ruin them all. She heard no such complaints that day at lunch though. This served to ease her mind for the moment. Perhaps it was nothing, she thought; she hoped. Sam was contemplating this over her meal when Bernie came to sit next to her.

"What has you brow so creased Sam?" he asked.

"Oh, I was just thinking about...you know...the Project" she said, attempting to seem casual.

"What about it?" he said.

"I think it's going well" she said "I was just imagining what we might find inside the structure."

"What do you think we might find?" he asked. Sam realized that she wasn't lying very well, but she stumbled on.

"Well there are probably...statues...or something. I really don't know, Bernie, that's why I was imagining it" she said, raising her eyebrows and giving a sarcastic bob of her head.

"Well what were you imaging was inside?" he asked, casually eating his lunch. Sam began to get angry that he was interrogating her. Really he was just innocently trying to make conversation.

"A pub, at least that's what I'm hoping for" she said in an irritated tone, and she got up and left.

Bernie laughed at this. Then, seeing that she was leaving he asked her where she was going and was very confused when she didn't answer. He hadn't noticed her irritation and assumed that she was just tired and so he returned his attention to his food.

Chapter 12

The midday climate created a rippling effect over the horizon. Without a cloud in the sky, the sun was unfiltered and burning bright. Everything appeared to have an orange tint to it as the rays of light bounced off the red sands of Mali. Except for the guard huts along the outer perimeter, there was nothing as far as the eye could see. Strangely enough this open landscape had a way of making a person feel trapped. The isolation of the camp was apparent when looking out over the miles of open desert. It was as if the site was a ship floating on a sea of sand and there was no land in sight.

The crew was taking a reprise from working in the heat of the day. After lunch, they had all dispersed back to their labs and tents. Some chose to work while others chose to nap. Sam had chosen to return to the dig site. It was her intention to ponder several matters that had arisen that day. She could think of no better place to deliberate than the sandy dunes of the dig site. The land appeared so calm under the African sky. She sat in a foldable camping chair and reviewed her reports that all of her GLs had presented to her on the current progress of the Project. There wasn't much to them considering that it was still the first day of the actual digging process. Most dealt with personnel and were all in all of a positive nature.

Dr. Maso Oasmi's report of the analysis of the stone samples that were taken upon arrival was consistent with the early analysis that Sam had seen before being sent out here. Osami had also presented another report on the shortcomings of the camp that he believed needed immediate attention. Sam shook her head as she read his complaints on, among other things, the taste of the drinking water and the unsanitary conditions of the showers. He also outlined a detailed criticism of buffet style serving, which included the many bacteria and viruses that humans could transmit through breathing and through touch.

Sam rubbed her head and sighed heavily. She got up from her chair and walked slowly back to her trailer office. There she found her students laughing and joking merrily with the two professional scientists on her staff. This served to brighten her mood a little. Pete had always been a little standoffish and it was nice to see him reveling with the others. She spoke with them briefly, then having placed her files back in her locked office; she retreated to her tent for a change of clothes.

It was still ten till two in the afternoon, which was forty minutes before the time that everyone was supposed to get back to work. Sam had no use for those forty minutes, so she decided to fill a water bottle, reapply sunscreen, and get back to the site. When she arrived she was surprised to find several others already there. Brad and Karissa were back to sweeping off the sand from the stone, and Rick was traipsing around taking measurements.

"Hello Dr. Byrne" said the two students as she approached them.

"It's okay to call me Sam," she said pleasantly. They smiled and continued sweeping. Sam seceded that she would join them; it had been a while since she had participated in what Pete called the 'menial tasks of Archeology'. Sam rather missed this part. While Pete might have considered it tedious, to Sam, it was what originally attracted her to Archeology. Her position now was loftier and therefore required less digging and more thinking. Whether it was menial or not, Sam still liked digging in the dirt. She grabbed one of the clearing brushes, which was essentially a broom with much softer bristles, and she set herself to sweeping.

Chapter 13

Rick held a small laser measuring device in his hand as he paced around the dig site. He recorded measurements in a small notebook that was very sandy at this point as he had dropped it several times. He had not been at all unaware of the Archeology students' laughing at him every time he did. He took out the notebook and made a note of the measurement that he had just taken. Then attempting to put the small pad back into his back pocket, he again dropped it into the sand. He looked over at the students as he picked it up for the eighth or ninth time. He was expecting to see them laughing at him, but instead he saw them sweeping alongside Samantha. He was pleasantly surprised by this. This was evidence that she wasn't as arrogant as perhaps he had first assessed her to be.

He completed his measurements and returned to the lab. There he found Chan and Shultz working hard at the computer models of the temple. Chris Martin was also there, and Rick greeted him.

"When did you get here?" He asked Chris

"I woke up from my nap about a half an hour ago" Chris responded.

"Are you going to be able to go back out there this afternoon?" asked Rick, who was concerned about the man's sunburn.

"I didn't think it was this bad earlier, but when I woke up from my nap..." he said pausing for effect.

"Did you try taking a nice cool shower?" asked Ira Shultz.

"Yeah, I tried, but even the water hurt my skin" answered Chris.

"Well, don't worry about the GPR, I'll go out there this afternoon, you need to stay out of the sun for a while." Rick placed the notebook on the table next to Chan and grabbed the hand GPR scanner and left the trailer again.

Chapter 14

The team worked through the scorching afternoon. The diggers were able to clear much of the sandy earth from the surface. Sam especially seemed pleased with their progress, but it was clear that everyone felt a sense of accomplishment. At five, the GLs left their people to oversee themselves and they made their way to the mess hall for their meeting. Sam thanked them all for their reports and asked how they felt about the first day. Everyone agreed that it was quite successful. Morale seemed to be high all around camp. In fact, that evening there were only two people who complained about anything. The first was Francois, who had taken issue with Margaret's smoking while he prepared the buffet. The second was Osami, who felt that there was a real problem concerning all the flies. Sam settled both disputes quickly. She simply told Francois that they would conduct their meetings in her office from now on and Maso that there was nothing she could do about the flies.

The next two days went as swimmingly as the first with the only real problems being a few malfunctioning AC units and a broken coffee brewer. The AC units were fixed by the maintenance team and Francois had found that the brewer worked just fine after he took it apart and put it back together again. The dig was going well also. They had managed to clear off the entire top of the structure and were just starting to dig down to clear the sides. The site now looked like a big sink hole with about four feet of temple emerging from the center of it. The onsite crew was pleased, as was Steve Philpot back in the states. Sam had been making regular reports to Philpot, who was a pretty harsh natured man, but he seemed satisfied by the news she was delivering.

It was the fourth day of digging that brought some serious issues. The day began with the showers being out of order, which put more than a few people into a foul mood from the get go. It seemed that something had gone wrong with the piping that ran the water from large tanks to the shower heads, and they were all spewing a dirty mixture of sandy soil and water. Several folks had resorted to dousing themselves with the drinking water to rinse off the muck that their morning shower had deposited all over them. Darrius had his entire team working on fixing the problem. There was a coffee shortage due to the coffee brewer being down again. Francois was attempting to compensate by offering people tea from his own personal stash.

As the day continued, the morale fell lower still. A sand storm had hit at about eleven o'clock, and had lasted until about two in the afternoon. Everyone was working to clean up the aftermath of the storm. The damage was minimal, but there were about three sleep tents that had suffered casualties. On top of that, they had lost a couple of folding chairs and a brush kit had disappeared beneath the sand. The wind had undone about a day's worth of digging by covering up a portion of the site with sand. The walking spaces between the trailers had to be cleared of some sand, and the mess hall needed to be thoroughly swept. A few people had complained of an excess of sand on the inside of their sleep tents, but Sam only reminded them that they were lucky to have one that was still standing. Sam was glad that PhilTech had consulted her before the Project was put into motion. It was not storm season in the desert, but there was always a risk of sans storms. She had recommended heavy duty tents with titanium framing that could withstand heavy winds. On top of that she made sure that they were anchored firmly to several steel rods that were buried deep in the earth. She patted herself on the back for the good call.

Towards the end of that awful day, there was one event that brightened their mood. At the five o'clock meeting, Rick had requested that they relocate themselves to the Tech Lab.

"You've got to see it to believe it," he had said to the group. Sam dismissed Darrius so that he could continue the cleanup efforts, and Amal had departed as well, having no local news of significance to report. Margaret, Bernie, Jake, Maso, and Sam followed Rick to the Tech lab where they found Chan and Shultz grinning gleefully.

"We have finally completed the three dimensional schematic of the structure" said Rick excitedly.

"Oooh, let's see it" said Margaret.

"Okay...this is the view from the top" said Rick clicking on the screen.

"My God" said Bernie with a deep breath.

"Christ, it's enormous!" cried Baxter.

"91 meters on each side at the base" said Rick bobbing his head in agreement.

"Let's see it in 3D," said Sam, giddy.

"It's also 91 feet tall," he said, clicking on the computer again.

"Shit!" cried Samantha as the image came up on the screen.

"What is it?" said Bernie. He was not expecting that type of reaction from Sam. Bernie was no Archeologist and was not sure what had Sam in a sudden tizzy. None of the crew was quite sure what had her eyes so wide at that moment. Margaret knew though.

"It's a ziggurat!" Margaret said with palpable enthusiasm.

"Cool" said Jake Baxter, shrugging a little.

"Cool? That's fucking amazing!" cried Sam.

"Okay, I'll buy it. Why is this so amazing?" said Bernie "we've seen dozens of ziggurats all over the world, what's so special about this one."

"It's the first. If our Radiocarbon dating is correct, and it is, this was built thousands of years before any other ziggurat in the world. It's the first ziggurat" said Margaret grinning.

"Okay, can someone please just tell me what the fuck a ziggurat is, cuz that looks like a pyramid to me" said Baxter.

"A ziggurat is basically just a steppe pyramid, you see how it has those sections that are tiered like a cake" explained Margaret.

"So...it's a pyramid," said Baxter.

"...sure" replied Margaret, realizing that there was no point to trying to explain further.

"This is so cool" said Bernie "the first ziggurat!"

"It's cooler than that" said Sam. They all silenced themselves and turned their attention to her.

"You're sure that this schematic is accurate?" she asked Night, who nodded enthusiastically.

"Then what we have here is truly amazing. This ziggurat is an exact match with the Etemenanki" said Sam. The faces looking back at her were blank.

"The ant man of sake? What did you say?" said Osami, joining the conversation after a long period of scratching his head.

"Etemenanki" Sam said again "it was a ziggurat in ancient Mesopotamia, it was torn down and rebuilt, and torn down again. Historians and Archeologists managed to put together a rough diagram of the original after finding a cuneiform tablet was found about seven years ago. I think I have a picture of the diagram in one of the books that I brought."

"When was this etema...what-ya-ma-call-it thing first built?" asked Bernie.

"Unknown" answered Sam. "No one's ever been able to come up with an exact timeframe, but it's thought to have been first built around 1400 BC. Etemenanki also shared the dimensions of our temple. This is so cool!" Sam laughed with delight.

"So our temple is the same as this 'atomic nun key' thing, just older. That still doesn't explain why PhilTech is so interested" said Baxter.

"Yeah, what exactly is their motive in funding this Project?" asked Chan.

"I think it's about time you explained that to us because I'm starting to feel like there's more to this story than we're being told" said Margaret. The rest of the group chimed in with similar complaints. Sam glanced briefly at Shultz who was giving her a glare of warning.

"Look, I'm sorry, but I simply can't say," Sam said, shrugging. The group, fortunately for Sam, took that to mean that she didn't know, and they dropped the subject for the moment. Sam was quite concerned by having been confronted in that manner. This keeping of the crew in the dark was becoming troublesome. She thanked Rick and the Tech crew for their hard work and fast results.

"You all did an excellent job, and Philpot will be pleased. I'll make my report to him tonight. Shultz, would you mind helping me with the video phone?" She said.

"Gladly" he answered.

"I'll be happy to assist you," said Rick with a slightly confused tone.

"Thank you, Rick, but Ira is perfectly capable of helping me. Anyway, you get a lot of sun today, so you should rest up for tomorrow." She said politely.

"Okay, sure. Thank you." He responded, still confused.

Chapter 15

After a delicious dinner that was voraciously consumed by the tired group of people, Rick made his way to his replacement sleep tent. His had unfortunately been one of the casualties of the day's sand storm. This new tent was the same as his previous one in every way, except, his original tent had been located on the outskirts of the camp site, and the replacement one was located right under one of the lights that lit the camp at night. Rick tossed and turned for some time before finally getting out of bed. He wished he could just turn off the bothersome light, but that wasn't an option. Ever since he was little he had always preferred absolute darkness when he slept. His mother had told him when he was five years old that he shouldn't be afraid of the dark, that monsters couldn't see in the dark so it was the perfect hiding place. Now, 26 years later it seems that he couldn't sleep at all without absolute darkness. He was no longer afraid of monsters; even then, the only monster that he really feared as a child was his abusive father, but his father was long dead after falling down the stairs one night. It turned out his dad couldn't see in the dark either.

Rick left his tent having decided to take a stroll around camp. He walked past the row of tents, past the bathroom facilities, and past the showers with their 'Now Working' sign taped on them. The mess hall had a few diggers inside. They didn't speak any English, so Rick saw no point in trying to converse with them and he continued around to the trailers, which all seemed deserted. The hour was around ten o'clock and everyone was in bed by now. The crew was very tired after their long day of hard labor under the African Sun.

Rick continued on the path that ran between the Chem. lab and the Wet lab, then between the Dry lab and the Tech lab. Since he was already awake anyway, he thought he'd get some work done so he rounded the corner of the Tech trailer. He was surprised to find the lights still on inside. Approaching the door, he became aware of voices coming from inside the lab. Instead of swiping his key, he listened for a moment. It wasn't his intention to eavesdrop, but he was intrigued by the conversation he had stumbled upon. The voices belonged to Samantha Byrne and Ira Shultz.

As he listened he noted that the tone of their conversation was quite angry. He leaned in close to the door in order to hear more clearly. He became aware of a third voice, it sounded very angry as well, livid even. He didn't recognize the voice, but came to find out that it belonged to Steve Philpot. The three of them seemed to be bickering about the Project. He wasn't able to pick up everything they said, but this is what he heard:

SAM: "You aren't here, Steve, you don't know how suspicious these people are getting, and they look to me for answers"

IRA: "They seem to think that you don't know any more than they do so what are you so worried about"

SAM: "I'm worried because I have to lie to everyone, it makes me very uncomfortable."

PHILPOT: "I don't give a shit about your moral qualms, Byrne"

SAM: "...(mumble mumble)...and anyway, they're gonna find out once we recover the artifact"

PHILPOT: "You just keep their attention on something else for now, Byrne, and then when you lay your hands on it, Ira here can bring it straight to me."

IRA: "That is the plan, and no one will ever find out about the artifact or what it does"

SAM: "...(mumble mumble)... I have to tell them"

PHILPOT: "You do and I'll not only fire you, I'll make sure that you never work in this field again.

IRA: "I'll keep a sharp eye on her sir"

PHILPOT: "Good"

SAM: "But..."

PHILPOT: "End of conversation! Philpot OUT!"

IRA: "I will be watching you Byrne ...(mumble mumble)...I will bury you"

SAM: "Fuck you asshole ...(mumble mumble)..."

IRA: "We'll see about that"

SAM: "Did your mother give birth to you or did you just fall out of your father's shithole? You know maybe if you pulled your head out of daddy's ass you'd realize what a little turd you really are."

Rick heard one of them get up and move toward the door. Not wanting to be caught he quickly ran around the far side of the trailer. From his hiding spot he was able to see Ira storm away towards the sleep tents. He waited for a while, but Sam did not come out. He decided to go in and check on her. He swiped his key card and slowly opened the door. Sam was sitting in a chair facing away from him; her head was buried in her hands.

"Go the fuck away!" she shouted without turning.

"Sorry, I'll go," said Rick. Sam suddenly turned around, her eyes wet with tears.

"Oh, Rick, I thought you were...someone else." She said, wiping away the evidence of her tears.

"Are you alright, it looks like you've been crying" he said.

"Crying?...no...it just..."

"Allergies?" he said, cutting her off before she could finish her lame falsehood. She laughed realizing that her intended excuse was very cliché.

"Okay, you caught me," she said smiling.

"Do you want to talk about it?" he said gently.

"I...I can't," she said with a very sincere quality.

"Want a drink?" he said, deciding not to press the matter.

"Yes!" Her answer was decisive and abrupt. Rick crossed the room to his desk and pulled a bottle of whiskey from a drawer.

"You keep a bottle of Bushmill's in your desk drawer" she said, realizing the irony.

"For medicinal use only" he said. "I don't have any glasses though, except the ones on my face." Sam laughed a little at his joke.

"Oh, you have had a rough night, that wasn't funny at all" he said. Sam laughed again.

"You have no idea how rough" she said, raising her eyebrows. They took a few swigs from the bottle.

"Actually, I do," he said after a moment.

"Do what?" she asked.

"You said I have no idea how rough your night has been. I have some idea" he said. Sam's face looked horrified.

"Explain" she said curtly.

"I kind of overheard some of your conversation with Ira," he said, confessing.

"Shit" she said "no one was meant to hear".

"I'm sorry, it was wrong of me," he said.

"How much did you hear?" she shouted, irate. Rick scratched his head, stalling for time.

"Tell me what you heard!" Sam asked again.

"I...heard a great deal about an artifact that we're here to recover and how you aren't supposed to tell anyone about it and..."

"Shit" she exclaimed, shaking her head.

"I won't tell anyone, really, I don't want you to lose your job" he said.

"I can't fucking believe this!" she said, her eyes widening.

"Maybe I shouldn't have mentioned it," Rick said. Sam looked at him for a second.

"No, it was good of you to let me know. You're a good person, an honest person. Not like me, I have to lie to my friends and colleagues every day just to keep my job. My God, what have I become...a corporate puppet to Steve Philpot? I'm his goddamn lap dog; I don't even like the guy. I mean what kind of fucked up person lies to his team, has *me* lie to the team, and even sends his own son to the middle of Mali to make sure that I'm lying properly." Her rant ended by her bursting into tears again. She managed to stop crying and took another drink from the bottle. Rick was silent. He actually hadn't realized when listening in, that Ira was actually Philpot's son. The conversation made a little more sense now that was cleared up.

"I'm sorry, I'm just...this is just too big, I have to tell everyone what's really going on here. It's just too big to keep secret" Sam said, clearly struggling with herself.

"Look, why don't you tell me everything, then I'll tell everyone. I'll just explain that I overheard it and that way Philpot can't hold you responsible" Rick said.

"That's sweet, but Philpot will still hold me responsible, and anyway I can't let you do that. It's something I have to do. Besides, what you overheard tonight isn't even the tip of the iceberg" said Sam. She took another big swig from the bottle, as did Rick.

"I'm going to bed," she said after a short while.

"Yeah, me too" agreed Rick, looking at his watch.

"Well" she said taking a deep breath in "tomorrow's meeting is going to be interesting." With that she left the trailer and went to bed.

Chapter 16

The fifth day was met with new fervor. The storm had put them behind schedule, but they were getting back on track now. Everyone got their coffee and headed to the dig site. They made excellent progress throughout the day. By lunch they had caught back up to where they were before the storm. In the afternoon, they made even more headway. At five, the GL meeting was called to order in Sam's office. They discussed several topics during the meeting but Sam had not yet revealed her secret. Rick was beginning to wonder if she had chickened out. He thought maybe she was just upset last night; maybe she didn't want to lose her job. He wouldn't think any less of her if she didn't tell them.

After everyone had discussed whatever particular issues they were having that day, Sam began to speak. Rick was very pleased that she was doing the right thing.

"Everyone, I have something to tell you all. This isn't easy for me to say, but bear with me. There's a lot of information that I'm about to tell you so, please just listen for now. Okay. I have not been completely honest with you all. I do know why PhilTech is funding this Project." There were gasps around the group, but Sam continued.

"This temple is spoken of in many ancient legends. Until it was found, it was believed to be a mythical place. There are Egyptian, Sumerian, Persian, Greek, and Roman folktales that all have similar stories about a place of the Gods in a faraway land. The Egyptians called this land Deshret, meaning red land. All the stories speak of a temple built long ago that contains an ancient treasure that was brought here by the Gods. We are here because PhilTech wants to get their hands on that treasure. Steve Philpot is so paranoid about someone taking his prize from him that he... He's going to fire me just for telling you about it." Several people cried out at this news. Sam took a deep breath and continued.

"So far, everything we have found points to truth in these ancient stories. Especially the age of the temple and the construction being similar to that of Etemenanki, which in Sumerian translates to 'the Foundation of Heaven and Earth.'"

"So what is this treasure? I mean are we talking about gold or..." asked Baxter.

"No, not gold, something far more valuable if the legends are true, and, like I said, so far they've been spot on. The treasure within the temple is supposed to be a magical device of the Gods. The texts are vague, as these ancient cultures probably didn't have the words or the understanding to describe it properly, but the artifact we're after...is believed to be...a time travel device."

"You're shitting me!" cried Baxter. Everyone reacted with either disbelief or laughter. Sam assured them that she was serious, and slowly they began to come around. Sam showed them the evidence from a file she produced from her locked desk drawer. Once everyone saw the solid evidence, they were convinced. The file contained the legends translated into English and a detailed report of the similarities of each of the legends. It also contained the carbon dating of the scripts that were found and the evidence linking the ancient cultures' Gods to Myths of travel between worlds, as it was translated.

They all stuttered and stammered in awe of the magnitude of what they were involved in. They asked many questions that Samantha did her best to answer in turn. They agreed that they would all be famous and that PhilTech would be stupidly rich if they held the secret to time travel. Everyone seemed to be satisfied by her divulgence of the facts.

She also made sure to inform them of Ira Shultz's true identity as Ira Steven Philpot, Jr., the son of their benefactor, Steve Philpot. She told them that he was sent there strictly as Philpot's spy and warned them to watch what they say around him.

"He's as slippery as an eel" she said, "so be mindful of your words when he's around"

"So are *we* supposed to keep this a secret now?" asked Bernie.

"Certainly not. I wouldn't ask you to lie to your staff like I have had to." Sam replied. "Just know that if Ira hears you say something, you can bet your boots that he's going to run and tell Steve about it."

"This is crazy. I can't believe we're actually talking about time travel. It's like a bad science fiction movie" said Baxter.

"What are we really saying here? Are we going to prove the existence of God or Gods or what? Because I'm an atheist. This could be very detrimental to my beliefs" Said Margaret comically, but she had actually touched on a serious matter.

"I ...I don't know, maybe." Sam had no real answer to her question. No one had an answer for her.

"I guess maybe we'll find out when we retrieve the artifact, but I can tell you that I believe firmly in the Bible and the existence of God" said Bernie.

"Well, for now, why don't we worry about getting some dinner?" said Rick, breaking the tension inside the room. They all headed to the mess hall together. That night, for the first time since arriving, they all sat together for dinner. They agreed it was nice to have meals together as a team and decided that they should perhaps do so more often.

Word spread quickly through the camp about the truth of the Project. Ira was livid and had screamed several times at Sam and the other GLs. They hardly cared, and that only served to darken his mood. It didn't take long for Ira to realize that his hold on Sam was fear based, and she was no longer afraid of what he could do to her. He had lost control of the situation; he no longer had power over the Project.

The group had a new found respect for Sam as a leader. They all knew how much she had risked in telling them about the device. There was nothing for it but to continue their work and wait for the other shoe to drop. To the surprise of everyone, it never seemed to drop. For two days they continued their efforts at the dig and made remarkable progress. Happily, Sam was still with them, she had not been fired.

Finally, she asked Ira what had made him change his mind about firing her.

"I haven't told dad" was his reply.

"That's...more noble than I believed you to be," said Sam.

"Yeah well, it's really more in my own interest than yours" he replied.

"I see; your father will hold you responsible too" she said.

"You know it" he said "he'll say that I've failed him and give that guilt crap".

"Well, for what it's worth, you've made a friend of me by not...tattling. Guess you're not a complete shit after all" said Sam, patting him on the back. He seemed unimpressed. He did, however, start to notice that people were sitting near him at meals again. Perhaps he had made more friends than just Sam.

Chapter 17

On the eighth bright, hot day of the dig, the crew uncovered the topmost door to the temple. It would be the first of three doors that the temple held in store for the crew, according to the diagram of Etemenanki that Sam had found in her book. The team worked tirelessly, clearing the sand and dirt from the doorway. Everyone was on pins and needles as the entrance to the temple was excavated. By the end of the day, it was fully accessible. Unfortunately, at that point, they were all exhausted so they reached the consensus that they would enter the temple at the start of the next day.

Though they hardly slept due to their excitement, they all managed to get up early in the morning of the ninth day. The excitement in the camp was palpable. Sam floated on air to the dig site that morning, but as she reached the sandy dunes of the dig, a very tired and very upset Jake Baxter stopped her in her tracks.

"Jake, you look like hell, what's wrong?" Sam asked.

"I haven't slept, the night patrol came and got me at about eleven last night." he said.

"What happened?" she asked.

"The Hummer came back, only this time, it was met by one or our Jeeps. A Jeep from camp, that wasn't signed out by anyone. Someone from camp stole the keys to a Jeep and had some kind of midnight rendezvous with your 'grave robber'. This could be really bad Sam. This is really bad. Someone from our team is a traitor." He was clearly disturbed as was Sam.

"It would seem, we traded one spy for another. Did you happen to see who was in the Jeep?" she asked.

"No, but I can tell you that whoever it was gave something to the Hummer. Papers I think" He said.

Sam's brow wrinkled. She touched the key around her neck. She thought back and couldn't think of a time when she had left her tent or her office or her desk unlocked. With the exception of the first day, but even then, it was for such a short period of time. She excused herself from the company of Jake Baxter and ran off toward camp.

She rushed to her office only to find that all of her files were in place, just as she had left them. What information had they given, and how on Earth did they get it. Her head was a jumble of questions. She decided that they shouldn't panic until they had more information, but Baxter was absolutely right; this was bad. Unfortunately there was nothing they could do about it right now, so there wasn't much to do but resume their work.

She got back to the dig site to find everyone was already there, and they were itching to get inside the ancient temple. It was still dark when Sam prepared to enter with the others, which included all the GLs, plus Jake, Sam's team, Margaret's team and Maso's team. They all wore masks to filter out any fine dust or mold spores as well as head lamps to better visibility. Maso wore a plastic, double lined suit that made him look like a CDC agent rather than a chemist.

"It's sealed so that nothing can come into contact with my skin or lungs," he explained. The group was used to his ways by now, and they only rolled their eyes.

They entered the door to the uppermost section of the temple. The inside was very dark and dusty. There was only a single large room with a low ceiling on this level. It was still breathtaking. The room began to look like a nightclub as their headlamps and flashlights twitched in all directions. The walls and ceiling to the large room were all heavily textured. Pete walked up close to a wall.

"Damn!" he exclaimed as he examined the wall. Karissa had noticed what Pete had exclaimed about at nearly the same time.

"It's writing!" she cried, excitedly.

"It's all over the place. Tiny writing everywhere!" Pete said.

"Amazing" said Margaret

"What language is it?" asked Maso.

"It looks like cuneiform. Am I right?" Sam said to Bernie.

"Yes and No" was his brief reply.

"Yes and No?" said Brad, attempting to get clarification.

"What the hell is that supposed to mean?" asked Jeremy, who was one of Margaret's support staff.

"Well, it is in the form of cuneiform, but it's not actually cuneiform. Cuneiform is written by pressing a wedged stick into wet clay. That seems to be the case here, but it's gibberish, it is not anything that makes any sense in the language. Thus my answer is yes and no."

"So you can't decipher it?" asked Sam.

"No way, I mean, it isn't a known language" Bernie replied.

"We'll just have to get someone out here who knows the language then" said Pete.

"You don't understand, man, this language...no one knows it. Cuneiform is the only language anyone knows of that is done in this fashion, and this isn't cuneiform" Bernie said.

The team was thrilled; it was just further evidence that this place was for real. They took many pictures of the writing and the room. They were careful to document everything extremely well. Sam was actually pleased to report the news to Philpot, who was, for the moment, quite pleased. That night, Sam threw a congratulatory surprise party for the entire group. They had music and alcohol and card games. Francois even went out of his way to bake a cake, though Sam couldn't figure out how as she hadn't told him ahead of time about the party. Somehow he just knew.

Chapter 18

Several more days passed and morale remained high despite the exceedingly hot days and long hours. By the eighteenth day of the dig they had opened the second doorway. This one led to two floors; the second and third levels from the top. These took longer to explore due to the increase in square footage, however, both floors were surprisingly empty. There were no clay pots, baskets, statues or offerings. For a temple of the Gods, it was shockingly sparse. In fact, there was absolutely nothing inside but a labyrinth of rooms and halls.

Samantha had asked the Tech group to take measurements in order to create a map. Several people had gotten lost inside the maze of the temple, including Margaret for several hours one day. She was finally found when she bumped into Jake. Jake was beginning to think that she liked bumping into him as it seemed to happen on a daily basis.

The team was a little discouraged by the lack of findings that the second door held for them, and yet they pressed on. The next door was going to take a while to get to. According to Sam's diagram, it lay at the fourth level from the top, and sat above the enormous base of the temple. The drawing showed a long, steep stairway that passed over the fifth, sixth, and seventh levels, counting from the top. Presumably, the doorway atop the outer stairway would lead to these levels. This suited the team just fine. Clearing away that much sand would have been problematic and the dig site was already becoming a deep pit.

Work continued day in and day out. The third door remained obscured by sand. Morale was rock bottom and productivity had slowed dramatically as a result. Even Sam was beginning to feel rather blue. On the twenty-first day of the dig Rick, Chris and Chan presented Sam with something to lift her spirits. They beckoned her to the Tech lab and showed her the completed map of the second and third levels.

"Good work guys" she said to them. They only grinned at her. She got the impression they were waiting for something.

"Really nice work" She said, thinking perhaps her previous statement was insufficient, but they only grinned wider.

"Okay I give up, why do you all look like the cat that ate the canary. The Cheshire cat at that, if you smiled any wider I think your heads would split in two." Sam awaited their explanation with one eyebrow raised.

"Look really closely" said Rick.

"Okay...what am I supposed to be seeing?" she asked.

"Ugh, look right here" said Rick pointing to the computer screen that contained the map.

"...it's a...it's a secret room" she said, finally seeing the inconsistency in the diagram.

"Eureka! She's got it" said Chan laughing.

"Don't worry, it took me a few minutes to catch it too" Chris said supportively.

"I'm going to get the team, we gotta check it out. Can we print off the map?" Sam said with fresh energy.

"Already done" replied Rick. Sam smiled a beautiful smile that made all the jaws of all the men in the room drop.

"Let's get going," she said joyfully.

Chapter 19

It was about one o'clock in the afternoon when they entered the temple. Rick, Sam, Margaret, Ira, Maso, Bernie and Jake made their way through the labyrinth. Having found the general location of the room that seemed to have no door, they began to search for an entry point. They searched for about half an hour with no luck until Margaret happened to light a cigarette.

"Look!" said Ira, pointing at the ceiling of the tunnel. In the crook of the ceiling and the wall, there was a small crack where smoke seemed to be drifting inward. The crack was at the top of a seam in the wall of the hallway. Normally this seam would have seemed innocuous, but here, it obviously lent credence to a secret and hidden chamber within the temple walls.

"The room has to be on the other side of this wall, and this seam might be some kind of doorway" said Sam.

"Great, but how do we open it?" said Baxter looking at Ira.

"I don't know. I found the crack, now it's your turn to figure something out" said Ira snappishly.

"Okay, well I could try busting through it, but somehow I don't think that would work" said Jake sarcastically.

"Hey!" said Maso, his voice muffled from inside his hazmat suit. They all turned to find him crouched on the floor, pointing.

"What is it?" asked Bernie.

"There's a tiny mark on the wall down here, it might be some kind of release for the door" he said.

"Where? I don't see anything" said Jake.

"Right here" Maso said, moving his pointed finger back and forth accidently tapping the symbol on the wall. Suddenly there was a whoosh as the hidden door rose to reveal the secret chamber within.

"Whoa" exclaimed Rick.

"That was cool!" said Baxter with a smile.

They shined their lights into the small chamber and entered apprehensively. Their lights fell on a pedestal in the center of the room. On top of the pedestal there was a small stand. Atop the stand was a spherical object, solid black and about the size of a softball.

"Jackpot! This has to be it" said Ira.

They stood frozen in awe as they began to realize that the sphere wasn't resting on the stand, it was hovering above it. As they stared, the sphere began to glow with an eerie tint. It was almost reflexive, almost iridescent, but definitely glowing. Maso reached out his hand to touch the orb. He was mesmerized, hypnotized by its strange beauty and mysterious hue.

They suddenly became aware of a noise that seemed to be pulsating through the tunnels of the temple.

"What is that?" said Sam.

"Sounds like...helicopters" said Baxter.

They all looked at each other for an instant before running back as fast as they could to the exit of the temple. The light from the open doorway was blinding and the noise from the choppers was deafening. They gazed into the sky to see no less than a fleet of helicopters descending on the camp.

"Friend or foe?" asked Sam

"There's no way to tell...yet," said Rick.

"We need to hide the device!" Ira blurted anxiously.

"We could just close the door again," said Margaret.

"Yeah, it took us long enough to find it, if they are unfriendly, we can convince them that there's nothing here and maybe they'll leave," said Bernie.

"No good, the maps are all on the computers" said Rick.

"We should hide it," Ira said again.

"Okay...okay let's do it" said Sam, making an on the fly decision.

"Um...Where's the Jap?" Baxter said as they turned around.

"Maso!" cried Margaret.

"He's not with us?" said Sam, alarmed.

"Maso!" they all began calling for him, but there was no reply.

"Oh dear, he must have touched that wretched time travel device" said Margaret fretting. "He's gone somewhere in time hasn't he?"

"No" said Jake dismissively.

The rest of the group was silent.

"That isn't really our theory is it?" He said

"No...he's probably just lost and can't hear us," Sam said. "Let's just go grab the device and hide it before whoever they are finds us.

"Agreed!" said Ira as they set at a run back to the secret room.

They returned to the room but had seen no sign of Dr. Maso Osami. The six were very sweaty and short of breath by this point. They all sort of leaned on each other out of exhaustion. Sam reached out to grab the device, but as she touched it, there was a strange feeling that began in her fingertips and spread throughout her entire body. It was a soft, fuzzy sort of feeling that calmed her frayed nerves and she felt at such peace. The warmth of this reaction made her think pleasantly of when she was little and she used to curl up with her grandmother under a blanket and sip cocoa by the fire on a cold winter night. It felt like happiness.

Part Two

Travelers

69

Chapter 20

S am became aware and alert after a brief but glorious period of that
fuzzy, warm feeling. She blinked heavily and shook her head,
realizing that she had somehow ended up on the ground. She ran her
fingers through the sandy cool soil as she got to her feet. She could
barely see in the darkness of the chamber, the only light being the dim
glow of the sphere. As she looked around she became aware that Bernie,
Jake, Margaret, Rick and Ira were in the room with her. Her head was
so muddled by the fuzzy feeling that had crept through her body. She
had never felt something so systematic; something that reverberated
throughout her whole being so thoroughly. She shook her head again
attempting to clear it of its fog. The others began to come around to
consciousness as well. She called out to them, but her voice was
surprisingly weak and sounded strained. She licked her lips, but her
mouth was dry.

"Sam..." she could hear the others. They sounded as weak as she felt.

"I'm here" she responded, groggily, "Bernie?"

"Here, Bernie here" he said, groaning. They all sounded off their
names in turn.

"What about Maso? Maso Osami, are you here?" asked Margaret.

There was no response to her calls for their Chemist friend. Each
of them got to their feet, rubbing the various parts of their bodies that
were sore from their apparent fall to the sandy stone of the temple floor.
They used their flashlights to look around, but saw no sign of Maso.

"He must have returned to camp" Sam said, the others agreed for
lack of a better explanation.

Rick began to make noises as though he were going to be sick.
A gurgling sound started in his stomach and traveled its way up to
his throat. He doubled himself over in a corner of the hidden room
and proceeded to purge himself of whatever was left of his lunch. His

colleagues, disgusted by this display of sickness, inquired politely as to his health, to which did not respond.

"What's up with the geek?" asked Baxter.

"He gets sick" said Bernie plainly.

"We were out for a while, my muscles are sore. Whatever that energy pulse was, it did a number on us all" said Sam.

"I don't hear helicopters, do you think they're in the camp?" asked Bernie.

"We can't let them get the artifact," said Ira with urgency.

"Well it's obvious that we won't be able to touch it to move it." Margaret said groaning and rubbing her head. "Some of us got the effects of the energy pulse *through* the others. Samantha was the only one actually touching it, and yet it knocked all of us out. It's obviously a very powerful form of energy, we shouldn't risk touching it again so soon, there may still be some residual energy in our bodies. We're lucky we didn't die or go into a coma or something" said Margaret.

"Well whatever it was it felt nice, I mean, before it knocked us all out" said Sam.

The others glared at her with spite. They had all felt the same full body energy, but what they had experienced was pain, not joy.

"You must have felt something different than the rest of us" said Bernie, disgruntled.

"Let's argue about it later, for now, let's get to camp and figure out what's going on there" said Jake.

"Good idea, I want to make sure Maso is alright" said Margaret.

"Rick, are you ok?" Sam asked him. He was still doubled over, leaning against the stone wall of the temple. He gave a lazy wave.

"I'll be along in a minute, go on ahead" he said choking and gagging.

They nodded, and cautiously began to make their way to the doorway of the temple. The heat from the sun hit them as they got close to the entrance. The temperature inside the shade of the temple was at least thirty degrees cooler than the outside. The bright light of day struck their eyes with a painful shock.

"Ack! It's bright" said Sam, covering her eyes.

"Increase that discomfort by about a thousand fold and you might be close to what we all felt all over when you touched the sphere in there" said Bernie.

"That's not what I felt..." Sam began, but was cut off by Ira.

"Don't you think it's weird?" Ira was looking at his wrist watch. "The helicopters landed at least thirty minutes ago, when we got knocked out, but there's no sign of them now" said Ira.

"Maybe they were friendly," said Baxter.

"Maybe...maybe we should take a look around," Sam said.

"What about Rick?" Bernie asked.

"He can catch up with us later, he's got the map so he shouldn't get lost," said Sam.

They made their way up the ladders of the multi layered dig site. They crossed over the sand, past the Guard Hut, and into the camp. There was not a person in sight. The camp seemed deserted for a moment. As they walked, they became aware that they could hear sounds of people in the mess hall. They headed directly there.

The sides of the mess hall were down, but they could hear the multitude of people that made up the rest of the team inside. They were able to discern that the topic under discussion was, not surprisingly, their disappearance. They were talking about very people who were about to enter the tent. Sam pushed the oilcloth side section aside and the five of them entered. Silence fell over the group inside the hall.

Pete was standing at the small podium in front of the group. He stopped mid sentence and stared at Sam and the others. His eyes were wide with amazement at seeing them standing there before them.

"My God," cried Pete in astonishment "where on earth have you been?"

"We went inside the temple to secure the artifact when those helicopters started to land, but it knocked us out with some kind of energy pulse" explained Sam.

"Helicopters? ...are you all alright?" inquired Pete who seemed very worried.

"We're fine now, Rick should be along any minute now, he wasn't feeling well" she responded. Pete's face seemed rather confused. He darted his eyes around the mess hall, then back to Sam.

"Rick...?" he asked, visibly baffled.

"Patrick Night...Tech geek" said Baxter attempting to clarify.

"Night is here" said Pete with raised eyebrows as Rick got to his feet from one of the picnic tables.

"Rick, how on Earth did you get back from the temple before us?" asked Ira.

"I...I don't know what you mean, I didn't go in with the five of you. I've been here all along" he said clearly confused. He glanced at Pete who returned his look of concern. They turned their attention back to the five.

"But...we left you...you were sick" said Sam.

She was very foggy still, so she glanced at her team for verification. They nodded in agreement with her statement. She looked back at Rick, and made a face of utter astonishment. Pete wrinkled his brow. He motioned for them to sit down, and then waved for one of the Medics to come over and take a look at the newly returned group.

"Could it be heat stroke or something?" he asked as Sarah Penn checked them out one by one. She tested the reactive response of their pupils to light, the reflexes in their joints, she even had them follow her finger as she moved it slowly from left to right.

"There doesn't seem to be any immediate sign of brain injury" she said "but I think we might want to get Paul and Roger in here". She was referring to Paul Fetzer and Roger Navarro, the other two Field Medics. She looked at Darrius who was standing with Pete behind her. Darrius nodded and left the tent to fetch them. Sarah turned her attention back to Sam. Her face betrayed her worry.

"You probably just need some rest, we just want to make sure we aren't missing anything before we let you go get some sleep" said Sarah, fulfilling her Nursly duty to make her patients feel safe.

"We're fine," said Sam resentfully.

"I'm sure you are. We just need to do some tests before we can say that for sure" Sarah said, smiling.

"Um...have you guys seen Maso? We lost touch with him before the energy pulse, we had hoped that he found his way back by now" said Margaret, looking around the mess hall.

"Who is this Maso?" asked Pete, shaking his head.

"Maso...always complaining, Maso Osami," said Baxter with an implied 'Duh'. Pete still seemed not to recognize the name.

"Maso Osami, Chemistry Group Leader" said Sam with a more fretful tone than she had intended to let on.

Pete and Sarah looked at each other with an unspoken exchange of worry. Darrius returned with Roger and Paul who were looking to Sarah for some sort of explanation. They seemed surprised to see that the five of them had returned.

"They show no sign of brain injury, but they are clearly confused. I found no bites or stings. It's possible that they may have suffered a slight concussion, though they don't seem to have any head injuries. They seem to believe that Night went into the temple with the rest of them, and they all insist upon the existence of someone named M...uh...uh"

"Maso Osami!" shouted Margaret angrily.

"That doesn't make any sense, why would they all have the same delusion? Even if they were suffering from heat stroke...You weren't stung by a scorpion were you?" asked Roger.

"I'd remember that," Bernie assured him.

"If it was a scorpion sting, they would be foaming at the mouth by now" said Paul Fetzer. "The scorpions around here that are venomous release a neurotoxin that will kill a person in just a few hours" he added, causing Bernie to shiver at the thought.

"We're not stung and it's no delusion, damn it! Maso!...He's our friend and colleague" said Sam angrily.

"I wouldn't say friend..." Jake teased. Sam shot him a look that seemed to say 'not now'.

"He's my friend!" Shouted Margaret "Everyone is acting like we are the crazy ones, meanwhile, we all know Maso, and know him to be missing. Now will someone please try and figure out what is going on here" said Margaret, jumping to her feet and storming out of the tent.

"Margaret, wait" cried Bernie, standing to go after her.

"You really should sit..." said Sarah.

She turned to go after Margaret, but as she pulled back the side of the tent, she gasped at what she saw. Outside the tent Margaret was speaking to Rick and telling him about the strange goings on inside. Sarah looked back at Night; the Night inside the mess hall. She looked back outside and made a small sort of noise that seemed to communicate her absolute confusion at what she saw outside the tent and what she knew to be inside the tent.

"What is it?" asked Pete, but Sarah didn't respond, she only sat down, trembling and staring off into space. From the outside, Margaret pulled aside the oilcloth flap that made up one of the sides of the mess hall and glanced around.

"Very well, if we are all crazies, I suppose *he* is just a figment of our imagination as well" she said motioning to Rick as he entered the hall beside her. There was a hush that fell over the room as everyone gazed back and forth between the two of them; the two Patrick Nights.

"I...um...I don't believe it" said Pete after a long period of silence.

"I think it's the device, the artifact. I think it does something other than time travel" said Ira.

"So what it duplicates people or something...Ooh, maybe it turned Maso into the other Rick..." said Jake.

"Yeah, and it erased everyone's memory except for our's, because we were all really changed too, we just don't know it," said Sam drolly.

"Do you think so!" said Jake in alarm.

"NO you idiot" said Bernie rolling his eyes.

"Fine...I don't hear any of you coming up with any theories," Jake said defensively.

"There has to be some sort of explanation," said Pete.

"I was thinking about the translation of some of the myths about our temple of the Gods" said Ira.

"And..." said Sam, waiting for him to make his point.

"I'm not sure, I would have to look at my notes," he said, getting up from his seat and leaving the tent at a run.

"While he's gone, why don't you explain some things to us?" said Darrius.

"Sure, we'll do our best," said Sam.

"Firstly, what was it you said about helicopters?" he asked.

"Right, that's why we ran into the temple in the first place, to retrieve the device so that whoever was coming in the helicopters couldn't steal it. You see, we found the device that PhilTech was looking for in a secret room in the temple" said Sam.

"*You* found the device!" exclaimed Pete.

"There were no helicopters. No one has been here since we opened the temple" said Darrius.

"But we saw them," said Bernie.

"None of this makes any sense, it's doing my head in" said Margaret rubbing her temples in frustration.

They continued to try to make heads or tails of their situation. The two parties seemed to be at odds with each other for some time. There were several inconsistencies between what the six of them recalled and what the rest of the people insisted was fact. Pete insisted that he had located the artifact days ago, and that there were never helicopters. Nobody knew who Maso was or even that he existed. On top of that,

Pete was certain that the five of them were hiding something. The only thing that the two parties did agree on was the strange existence of two Ricks. Suddenly Ira burst back into the mess hall with files in his hands. He was white as a ghost.

"I think I can shed some light on our situation," he said, breathing heavily.

"It's about damn time someone explained," said Jake.

"Listen…I've looked back through my files, and I've found that the language in the ancient myths about this place is somewhat…vague. I believe we've misinterpreted it." Ira paused a moment and opened one of his folders, and then continued. "Here, where the Egyptian myth describes the place as 'the gateway to the Gods…wherein there is a doorway to that which is known only to the Gods…a portal to that which is unseen to mortals…times unknown'. That's pretty vague, but the Sumerian Myth uses nearly the exact same terminology. This is what the Sumerian one said" He leafed through the pages in his files and then continued "It says: 'The place of Gods…where heaven and Earth collide…where the Gods may travel through the door to times unknown.'" He paused to absorb the information, and then continued to make his point. "They all use nearly the same words that our experts at PhilTech thought were describing time travel. But what if the phrase 'times' meant…instance rather than actual time. What if the translation was inaccurate and what if what we're actually dealing with here is unknown instances." The look on Ira's face was that of a great epiphany. He seemed very excited, but the others were not yet with him. He shook his head and continued.

"What if the device isn't a time travel device, but a…reality travel device" he said.

There was a silence that fell over the entire group. Sam was in a state of absolute disbelief.

"You think that we are in an alternate reality…a…parallel universe?" said Sam, raising her eyebrows.

"Exactly" said Ira. "It explains everything." He shut his file and handed it to Sam who began to flip through it.

"But aren't there infinite realities, how is it that we've ended up in one that is nearly identical to what we know as reality" asked the Rick that had joined them originally.

"I...I don't know," answered Ira. His face had taken on a stern, contemplative expression.

"How do we get back, is this...door, the sphere, I mean, does it only go to the two places, or...or what?" asked Sam.

"I...uh..." Ira stuttered, shaking his head slightly.

"You don't know do you?" said Jake.

"Lay off him already!" said Bernie, "He's told us more than we knew before, so let's just try and figure this thing out together rather than assuming he magically has all the answers."

"Thank you" said Ira, taking a deep breath, "here's what I can tell you...I think that when we touched the device, we...we changed reality. All of us who were either touching the device, or touching someone in contact with it, were made immune to the effects of the shift.

"So we need to figure out how to shift reality back to how we know it," said Sam, cocking her head to the side, thoughtfully.

"That would be great, if we knew how to do that," said Bernie.

"Maybe there's an instruction manual" said Jake, sarcastically.

"Sure there is, but no one can read it," said Margaret.

They looked at her for a moment.

"The writing in the uppermost chamber!" exclaimed Bernie pointing at her as she nodded.

"How does that help us?" said Rick.

"It doesn't," said Jake, crossing his arms and shaking his head.

"Would you mind not being so...*you* for a moment, Baxter" said Rick.

"You...don't know about the program," said Pete.

"Program?" said Rick.

"Can you decipher the language of the chamber on the top of our temple?" asked Sam.

"Night...that is, our Night has...is trying to put it through a decryption program that he created" said Pete.

Night, the Night that was local to this new reality, looked at Pete oddly. Sam took note, but wasn't sure what it was about.

"This is excellent news," said Rick.

Sam got her feet, followed by the others. She turned to stand in front of her team. She thought for a moment before deciding how she was going to delegate the work that needed to be done.

"Ira, Bernie, Rick and...other Rick, you work together to get that language translated. Pete, you're with me. We'll get the team together and try to search the lower levels of the temple. There may be something there that can help us. Margaret, your team will join ours to search the temple. Jake, your job is to help out whoever needs an extra hand around here." Samantha finished speaking, and turned to leave the tent in order to begin working.

"Just a minute!" said Pete, before anyone could leave "Just who exactly put you in charge?"

"Well, I am in charge, being the PM and all." She looked at his stern, unhappy face. "Do you take issue with something I've said, Pete?" she asked.

"Yeah, I'm the PM around here, and if anyone is going to give orders, it's going to be me," he said demandingly. Sam inhaled deeply and slowly. She hadn't anticipated this difference between their two realities. The whole idea was a bit odd to everyone on both teams. Her team was used to her style of leadership, whereas Pete's team was used to his style. There was a brief silence before Sam spoke again.

"You *did* offer to help," she said gently to Pete.

"Yeah, I meant that you could sleep here and we would feed you while Night's program is working on the translation. That is all I meant" said Pete curtly.

"You aren't going to let us help?" said Sam, shocked.

"This is my Project, you aren't in charge, I'm in charge and I don't want you and your incredible team stealing my glory by cracking this code we've found" he said coldly.

"We don't want to steal anything, we just want to go home!" cried Margaret.

"By your own admission, you touched the device while attempting to hide it" he said.

"Not from you, not from our colleagues and friends!" said Sam, feeling very under attack.

"I've suspected for some time that you might be trying to take the device for your own personal gain, Sam. Your disappearance has only served to confirm it" Pete said.

"I'm not *your* Sam, I'm a different Sam from a different reality, and I'm telling you that our only motive here is to put reality back to how we know it" pleaded Samantha.

"Which would destroy reality as we know it" said the other Night.

"I'm sorry, but I can't let you be a part of this Project. Your key cards will be locked out of all secure areas. You are limited to observers only" said Pete with a cocky smile.

"This is bullshit!" shouted Jake as several guards surrounded them.

His protestations were joined by the rest of the travelers, but their complaints fell on deaf ears. The team of this new reality seemed to look at them as untrustworthy and suspicious. Their key cards were taken from them by force along with their masks and gear with the explanation that if they didn't have the gear to enter the temple, they would be less likely to go snooping around in there. Jake managed to conceal his sidearm from his former guard team, Sam and her team members were shown to a replacement tent. They were told that after the storm, they were left with only one spare tent. They were to spend their time here.

In their tent they quietly and furtively discussed their present predicament, and tried to come up with potential ways of reasoning with their friends turned enemies. They were clearly being held in great suspicion. Their tent was being carefully watched over by several guards. For this reason, they spoke to each other in hushed tones. Sam and Margaret had attempted to get a cup of water from the water tent, which had only served to raise the suspicion of the pacing guards outside. They were told that water would be brought to them, but that they were not to leave the tent. Feeling very defeated the two ladies had gone back inside the sleep tent with the others.

The unfortunate result of their water request was that the guards were now pacing in closer proximity to the tent. They were sure that they were being listened to as they spoke of their quandary. Discussion of their situation was necessary, so the resulting suspicion was unfortunately unavoidable. As for water, they were painfully aware that they were prisoners when the much needed hydration hadn't been provided. Out here, in the Sahara, water was necessary to survival. They had all been made to take a survival course before being shipped off to the middle of Mali, and the number one, underlined rule of survival in the Sahara was water. Still, it did not come.

Trapped in the tent, they talked over the possibility of shifts in reality. They attempted to explain to Jake the finer points of the theory of alternate realities, but having no background in science whatsoever, they were forced to start at the beginning.

"So, reality is everything that we perceive as such, but there are infinite realities. It is theorized that if you can conceive of something, there is a reality that supports it." said Margaret.

"So is it a reality because you think it or do you think it because it's a reality?" asked Jake.

"Well...Yes" said Margaret, squinting her eyes.

"I don't get it," he said.

"God your dumb, it a good thing your nice to look at" Margaret said, laughing.

"I think you're confusing him" said Bernie "all you really need to know is that there are more realities in existence than we can count."

"All of them exist simultaneously" added Rick.

"And, though some may be extremely similar, there are no two of them alike" chimed in Sam.

"So...some of them are really close to what we know as reality, and some are fuck nuts crazy compared to ours" said Jake.

"Eureka!" said Margaret, putting her hands in the air with relief.

"So we're in one of the crazy ones right, cuz everything's all fucked up, right?" Jake said nodding enthusiastically. The rest of the team sighed with frustration.

"No, actually this one's very close to ours considering...well considering how many factors there are in the universe. This one is uncannily close to ours" said Ira.

"Great" said Jake sarcastically, his spirits lowering.

"Actually I've been thinking about it and I think that rather than changing our reality, that we've actually...physically been transported to an alternate one. Which is a considerably better situation than I previously thought" Ira said.

"That makes sense, with Maso disappearing and all," said Margaret.

"What have we discovered?" said Jake, shrugging and still confused.

"Because Maso disappeared first, but we still knew of his existence, that means that the sphere transports people to alternate realities, rather than changing the current reality." said Sam, who was having no problem keeping up with Ira.

"Whaa?" said Jake, whose face was beginning to twist with perplexity.

"Maso disappeared, this indicates that he was actually transported somewhere else" said Rick.

"If reality changed, we wouldn't know he existed after he disappeared, just like these people don't know him because he was never here in this reality" added Sam.

"Sure" said Jake bobbing his head, but it was clear that this discussion was outside of his understanding.

"That's good, though, because we know that our home...our native reality is out there somewhere" said Rick.

"What's also good is that we know it can be controlled somehow," said Ira.

"How do you know that?" asked Sam.

"Well...the legends of these ancient cultures all indicate that the so called Gods used it to travel. Travel implies that they left and then returned, rather than just disappearing forever, thus there must be some way of returning to our home reality" said Ira.

"But...but they must have disappeared, because we don't believe in those Gods now" said Margaret.

"...True" said Ira "but if each of these cultures knew of this place, and knew the Gods used it to travel, then the reality of those who used it wasn't changed" he said.

"Great, so how do we use it?" said Bernie.

"There's no buttons, no markings, no levers, no mechanisms whatsoever anywhere in the chamber" said Margaret.

The group kicked around theories and ideas until they finally decided that it was something that they couldn't just guess at, they would need that translation of the writing in the uppermost room of the ziggurat if they were going to really understand what was going on here. Ultimately what it came down to was that they would just need more information altogether before they could form any real idea of how the device worked.

Chapter 21

At six o'clock that evening, they emerged from the tent for dinner. Before they could get out of the tent they were stopped by a guard who informed them that plates or food would be brought to them. Remembering his promise of the water that never came, they were less than convinced. Feeling more and more like prisoners of their own team, they re-entered the tent. They discussed the prospect of breaking into the Tech lab to try and glimpse the translation, but it didn't take long for them to realize that it wouldn't work.

"Even in our reality I wouldn't leave the program running unless I was there to keep an eye on it" said Rick. "And when I'm not there I've got multiple pass codes that protect any files that have to deal with the Project. Even if I have similar passwords here, it could take a while to guess at" He added.

They decided that security was too tight to risk an attempt at espionage. They were beginning to feel somewhat hopeless. Eventually they were met by a friendly face that happened to pop in on them. It was around seven thirty when Francois wheeled a cart of food into their tent. He said something in another language and formed a big smile on his face. Bernie laughed and translated Francois's words.

"Anybody interested in going home?" Bernie translated, happily.

A hearty "Yes" was their collective response. Francois spoke at length with Bernie translating energetically. He explained that Pete had been lying to them all along. The deciphering of the language from the temple was already complete and that it had been sent to Steve Philpot along with all records of it which were subsequently erased from Night's computer memory. He went on to say that they were to be studied as evidence of the device's power. Pete and his crew were working on a way to transport the device along with Sam's team to a PhilTech laboratory facility in the states. The true reason they were being held prisoner was because they were to be guinea pigs of PhilTech.

The group was greatly disturbed by what they were hearing from their old friend. Finally Francois said something that gave them hope.

"I have a plan for getting you back to the Orb" he said, as translated by Bernie.

"How, please!" said Sam excitedly.

They all twittered with excitement at the thought of a daring escape. The chance to save themselves from a fate of being poked and prodded by PhilTech scientists was thrilling, and frightening. Francois explained that it would be risky, but once they were at the Orb, they could use it to travel again. He added that getting home would be entirely up to them.

"How do you know all of this?" asked Rick.

"He's Francois, he knows everything," said Bernie laughing.

"So what's the plan?" asked Sam.

Francois cocked a sideways smile and said that he would cause a distraction that would occupy everyone's attention while they escaped to the temple.

"Simple but effective" Bernie said for Francois.

"Indeed" said Margaret.

"Will it work though?" asked Sam.

"They will all come running when..." Bernie stopped mid-translated-sentence. He looked at Francois in alarm.

"Allumer?" said Bernie to Francois in French.

"When what!" asked Jake.

"Francois plans to set fire to the camp" said Bernie, "he said nobody will get hurt, it'll just be a distraction".

"That's crazy!" said Sam.

"Yeah, but it might be our only chance," said Ira.

Sam thought for a moment, clearly struggling with her conscience. Finally, she agreed with Francois that it was the only way. Francois smiled as there was shouting from outside the tent.

"You sly bastard, you already started the fire" said Bernie. Francois only kept smiling as a reply. He ushered them out of the tent. He then told them all to hurry up and get home.

"I don't suppose you know how we might do that?" Sam asked Francois, but he only smiled more. Then to everyone's surprise, including Bernie's he spoke again, this time in perfect English.

"As I said before, getting home is entirely up to you" he grinned and gave a slight nod.

Sam and Bernie stared at him in awe. Neither of them was aware that he could speak English. Furthermore, they were confused by the fact that he had waited until now to reveal this fact, and that he chose such a disappointing thing to say. Before they could say another word to Francois, they were pulled by the arms out of the tent by Jake and Rick. They ran quickly, following closely behind Margaret and Ira. The six of them ran full throttle at the dig site. It wasn't long before some guards took notice of their improved escape and gave chase. Luckily, the team knew the labyrinth of the second level better than the guards that pursued them. They were able to make it back to the sphere without being caught. Having very little time to discuss their plan of action, they quickly decided that they would all touch Sam, and she would touch the sphere as before. Their hope was that it would work like it had before, only in reverse this time, taking them home. The six were then overcome once more by the energy of the device.

The pain buzzed in their bones as they made the jump from one reality to the next. Sam was once again overcome by the feeling of soft joy, but the others felt the same pain from before, perhaps slightly lessened. The energy of the device wore off after only a few minutes, though. They became aware of their surroundings in what seemed to be a darkened museum exhibit. It didn't take them very long to realize that they were stuck behind a large piece of glass that separated them from the rest of the displays of the museum. Though they were glad to have escaped from the clutches of Pete and the rest of their team, they were less than thrilled at being trapped in an exhibit. They were also rather perturbed at being trapped in their current display with Rick who had gotten a little sick again and had thrown up in the corner on a wax statue of a man who was dressed as some sort of priest or ceremonial figure.

The false person was wearing robes and jewelry that seemed to be made to look like the material that the Orb, as Francois had called it, was made of. There were other wax figures here too that appeared to be dressed almost as early Egyptians dressed. They wore skirts and loin cloths and more fake jewelry. All the wax figures were positioned around the Orb in the center of the display. The Orb seemed to be the only thing in the display that was the genuine article, everything else was a reproduction or fabrication.

This exhibit was exciting, although they knew that they weren't home; there was the possibility that someone here in this new reality might know more about the Orb than they currently did. They banged on the glass that separated them from the rest of the museum to try to get someone's attention, but there was no one there. It was nearly eight o'clock and it was Sunday, they presumed that the Museum was closed.

"Well we clearly aren't home" said Ira.

"We've been gone for half a day, it's possible that whoever was in those helicopters might have gotten us to the Cairo Museum of Antiquities by now, especially if they were Egyptian" Sam pointed out.

"This is definitely the Cairo Museum," said Margaret.

"How do you know?" asked Jake.

"I held the title of curator here for two years, we're in exhibit number fourteen. When I worked here it was wax sculptures of King Tut and Hatshepsut" she said.

"Great...so how do we get out of here?" said Jake.

"Oh, we're sealed in without a key," she said pointing to the door on the back wall of the display. It was painted to blend in with the backdrop scenery of the exhibit and the others hadn't seen it before she pointed directly at it. It was well camouflaged, but there was a tiny keyhole below a small handle on the door. The handle and the lock looked rather antiquated compared to the rest of the modern style Museum, but it proved quite strong as they tried fruitlessly to bash through the door. Finally, they decided that there was no use in trying to break out of the exhibit.

They felt an overwhelming sense of being powerless as they sat in the enclosure. Sam had run her fingers along the back wall as if somehow the feel of the paint might give her better understanding of their current placement. Unfortunately, the eggshell surface of the painted sky had not divulged any of its secrets to her.

"We can get out in the morning, right?" said Sam to Margaret, who was their resident expert on the Cairo Museum.

"Sure, someone should be along at some point tonight, but if not, there will be someone coming along in the morning for sure" Margaret said.

The team seemed less than convinced and continued their efforts of banging on the glass hoping to rouse a security guard or night watchman. The noise on the inside was a reverberating bong, but there was no telling what it sounded like to the outside. They shouted and banged with all their hope. Still, no one came and they were forced to spend the night in the enclosure. They maintained their optimism that they were home though.

As they took their places for sleep, the dire weight of their situation set in. Sam had never been forced to spend the night in a place that wasn't meant for sleeping. The most obscure place that she had ever slept was the couch, and now here she was sleeping on a floor of straw and plastic grass. Her bedfellow was a wax, Neolithic, Malian Orb worshiper. As far as she was concerned, their situation was as bad as it could get. She stared at the wax feet until she fell asleep.

Come morning, someone opened the exhibit, and as a result, they were released. The person who had opened the door was a woman with beautiful brown skin and a blue lab coat. She seemed very alarmed at having let living people out from her wax display. She was so surprised that she seemed to be speechless.

"Thanks" Sam said to her, for lack of a believable explanation.

"Sure...who are you?" she said.

"Oh...we sort of..." Sam began.

"We came from the Orb thing in there," said Bernie.

"Oh...okay" said the woman, oddly paying them little mind. She wants about her duties within the display ignoring their presence altogether.

Sam and the others thought it was strange that the woman was so indifferent to their arrival as well as their mention of how they had arrived. Rick was a little sympathetic to her as he had made a bit of a mess in one of the corners of the exhibit. He made a point of apologizing to her as they passed one another in the enclosure. The six left her company and continued on through the Museum where they hoped to find some information about the Orb and how it worked. They wandered through the museum trying to find someone who was in charge, or at least someone who would listen to their plight. They found no such person right away. It took them hours to locate someone in authority as no one seemed to want to listen to them. Finally they managed to stumble upon the curator of the Museum. The man was standing cross armed in the center of an alleyway between two rooms of exhibits. He seemed to be surveying the many people who were now milling around the Museum.

"Hallo," said Bernie, cheerfully.

"Hello," the man said.

"Are you the curator of this museum?" said Sam.

"Yes Ma'am, what can I do for you today?" said the man.

"Um...we came from the Orb...we used it to travel here from another reality" said Sam trying the honest approach. It had seemed to work with the lady in the blue lab coat at the exhibit, so Sam was hoping that her honesty would be appreciated here as well. Sometimes there was truth in the old adage that the truth shall set you free.

"That's not my department," said the curator.

It was certainly not the response that any of them expected. Rick had thought that it was generally a peculiar thing to say, but in this context, it was particularly odd. He leaned over to say as much to the others, but their faces clearly read that their reaction to the man's words was similar to Rick's.

"Okay...so...who do we talk to about using the Orb to get home?" Sam said loudly and slowly.

"What is this matter concerning?" said the curator.

"We want to fucking get home, man" shouted Bernie.

"Yeah, who the fuck do we see about getting home?" yelled Jake.

"I'm sorry, but homes and houses are not my specialty" said the curator.

"The Orb!" said Sam, "how do we use the Orb"?

"The function and use of all artifacts is under the jurisdiction of the artifact manager" said the curator.

"Come on...I think I know where we can find some answers," said Margaret, frustrated.

They stormed off following Margaret down a set of stairs to the basement of the museum. The hallway was narrow but well lit and beautifully decorated in ancient Egyptian style. The fake hieroglyphs on the wall read letters and random names the Bernie presumed were ill-scribed by the painters of the renovated section that they were now in. They stopped in the basement level in front of a large iron gate that separated the Museum from the behind the scenes section.

Margaret called out for someone for a few minutes and intermittently banged on the iron until finally someone came to the gate. The man was dressed as the woman from the exhibit this morning, wearing a blue lab coat and khaki pants. He said something in Egyptian, then realizing that the group was speaking English; he spoke again in their tongue.

"Can I help you with something?" he said.

"Yes actually, you can," said Margaret.

"Do you have a blue slip?" he said.

"Um...No...just listen, the Orb in exhibit fourteen, what do you know about it?" she said.

"I'm sorry, I can't help you unless you have a blue slip" he said curtly.

"We just have a question about the Orb," said Sam.

"All questions are to be directed to Customer Service near the entrance of the museum" said the man, and then he walked away.

"Wait...we just want to know..." but the man did not stop; he disappeared from sight around a corner.

"Well, I guess we have to go to Customer Service" said Rick sighing loudly.

"Follow me, I know the way," said Margaret.

She led them back up the staircase to the main section of the museum again. They arrived at the customer service desk near the entrance. They were disheartened to find a line that led nearly all the way outside. Taking their place at the end, they felt very displeased by their present situation. The end of the line placed them backed up against the turnabouts at the entrance and they could feel the heat from the morning sun radiating through the wood and glass of the doors. They pleaded with the people in line in front of them saying that they were pressed for time and they only had one question, but no one would pay heed. Their wait in the long line was lengthy before they finally stepped up to the counter of the Customer Service Desk that was so marked. The woman who sat at the desk was pretty with smooth brown skin and long black hair. She seemed a bit humorless, but Sam supposed that she was just having a bad day. She hoped that if she was charismatic, they might get the answers they required.

"Can I help you?" said the lady behind the counter dully.

"Yes, we have a question about exhibit number..." said Sam forgetting the number of the exhibit momentarily.

"Number Fourteen. The Orb from Mali" said Margaret smiling.

"I need to see two forms of ID and your entry stamp" said the dull lady behind the desk.

"Here's my ID" said Jake, charmingly "and I'll be glad to show you my stamp later" he said winking and smiling at the lady behind the counter.

"I need to see your stamp now sir" she said humorlessly.

"We...um don't have a stamp, may we purchase one here?" said Sam, faking a smile in spite of her frustration.

"I'm sorry, all stamps must be purchased outside before entry...NEXT!" she said.

"But wait, we waited so long..." said Rick, but the people behind them were already pushing and shoving them out of the way.

The team went outside to wait in the long line for the entry stamps. Margaret was not terribly upset because she had been wanting a cigarette for quite some time now. She pulled a fresh pack from her pocket and packed it against her hand. Jake noticed that as she opened it, she turned one upside down. Having formerly been a smoker while he was in the Army, he recognized it as a 'lucky cigarette', a sort of superstition among smokers.

He watched her as she lit the end of until it glowed thoroughly, then she exhaled the billowing smoke from between her lips with a sigh. Her eyes closed as the fresh nicotine coursed through her blood. She opened her eyes and noticed that Jake was staring at her intently.

"Do you want one?" she asked, flipping the pack open and pointing it toward Jake.

"No, thank you I quit a long time ago" he said, taking one anyway.

She laughed and leaned over to light it for him with half a smile at having corrupted a reformed smoker.

"I noticed you turned up a lucky" he said, referring to the upside down cigarette in the pack.

"I usually don't" said Margaret, blowing smoke out of her mouth again "but I figured we could use all the help we can get".

They waited for another hour and a half in the hot sun on the steps of the Museum. The line progressed until they eventually got to the man distributing the stamps. They were hot, sweaty, sunburned and ill tempered by the point that they were finally able to get their stamps for entry.

"How many?" he said in a dull and bored tone.

"Six" answered Jake.

"American?...hmm...It's 28 dollars American per person to get in so for six that's...162 dollars, American" he said.

"It's 168, moron!" said Margaret.

"Margaret!" said Sam, raising her eyebrows at her colleague.

"What...his math was wrong!" Margaret said, shrugging.

Sam shook her head and paid the man in cash, muttering something about the price being outrageous.

"All complaints must be registered at the Customer Service Desk. Here are your stamps. Thank you, have a nice day" he said as he stamped all of their hands. The team proceeded back into the museum, exasperated by the hoops they had been made to jump through.

"Is it always this bad" asked Jake.

"No...either they've implemented new policies, or this isn't our reality" said Margaret.

"I'm betting that this isn't our reality," said Sam.

They waited in line again at the Customer Service Desk for another two hours before seeing the same pretty lady from before. The woman's dull, joyless face changed into a pleasant smile as they approached. For a moment Sam thought that she might have recognized them from before and perhaps she might be more agreeable this time around. They stepped forward to the counter and to their great disappointment; she placed a sign on her desk that said "out for lunch". Sam protested, but the woman only smiled and happily told them that she was on her lunch break and that she would be back in thirty minutes. They sighed heavily and awaited her replacement, but none came. Half an hour later, on the dot, she returned to her counter.

"We have our stamps now!" said Sam trying to be pleasant, though she was extremely pissed off.

"Stamps are given upon entry, please go outside to get your stamps" she replied. "NEXT" she shouted.

"Wait...we have our stamps, and we have a question" shouted Rick.

The people in line behind them began to push them aside as the others had done before. This time Rick and his friends pushed back. They were tired and angry and they were not about to lose their place in line. They had a fresh sense of determination and a growing sense of rebellion.

"Please wait your turn" said the lady behind the desk to the next in line. "Can I help you?" she said looking at the six of them again.

"Yes, we have a question about..." said Sam.

"...about exhibit number thirteen" said Rick.

"Number fourteen!" said Margaret, correcting him.

"All questions about exhibits must be directed to the exhibit manager. The Exhibit manager for number thirteen is..." she began.

"For number fourteen!" shouted Margaret.

"The Exhibit Manager for number fourteen is in office number 310. His office is located on the third floor" she said, giving them a green slip of paper.

"Thanks," said Sam.

"Thank you" said Jake to the woman almost as though he was speaking to a sheep.

Sam examined the green piece of paper that the woman had handed to her. It said: "Question; customer" then on the next line it said: "Specific Question concerning exhibits currently on display" and below that: "exhibit number" beside which the woman had penciled in the number 14. They walked away from the desk and followed Margaret up a flight of stairs. She explained that in reality, the elevator was nearly always broken, so the stairs were the most efficient way of getting around. They ended up on the third floor outside an office with a thick wooden door marked 310 in gold numbers.

"Here we are," said Margaret, knocking on the door. There was no answer.

"Maybe he's at lunch," said Ira, knocking again. The door opened to reveal a plump man with brown skin and grey hair standing in the entrance of his tiny office. He was wearing a blazer and a tie with denim jeans and white sneakers. He looked like a professor that Sam had in under-grad school, except her professor had been quite jovial compared to the man before them who was wearing a sour expression.

"Can I help you?" he said in Egyptian.

"We have a question about exhibit number fourteen," said Sam, in English.

"Do you have an appointment?" he said, now speaking English.

"...We have a green slip" said Sam, holding up the paper.

"Please take your green slip to the receptionist to make an appointment" he said shutting the door"

Angered, the team made their way to the receptionist's desk to make their appointment. Her kiosk was in the middle of the third floor where three other long hallways made and intersection. Sam handed over the green slip to the receptionist. The woman opened a large book and began to flip through the pages. The team was incensed to find that his schedule wasn't open for appointment for another three weeks.

"Fuck this" shouted Jake slamming his hand on the reception desk. He huffed as he headed down the hall again to office number 310. He shoved open the wooden door and barged in.

"We have a question about exhibit number thirteen" Jake shouted at the man who was now sitting at his desk inside the office.

"Exhibit number thirteen is not my department" the man said without looking up.

"Number Fourteen!" shouted Margaret.

"Do you have an appointment?" he asked, finally looking at them.

"Yes, it's for right now, mother fucker" shouted Jake.

"Sorry, it's been a trying day, what with all the lines" said Sam, still attempting to maintain diplomacy.

"All complaints are to be taken to the Customer Service Desk" said the grey haired man.

"No...we have a question, not a complaint" said Bernie.

"Do you have an appointment?" he asked again.

"Yes, it's for 12:45 today" said Ira, glancing at his watch.

"Please wait for the time of your appointment" he said, looking at his clock and then back down at the papers on his desk.

The team stood in silence for the three minutes until the clock rolled over to exactly 12:45 in the afternoon. Sam had to consciously work to keep her foot from tapping impatiently on the linoleum floor. Bernie was drumming his fingers on the door frame while Jake simply stared at the man for the duration of the three minutes. After what seemed like an eternity, the hands on the clock finally read that the time was now 12:45. The grey haired Exhibit Manager brightly greeted them at that time and asked if he could help them. His sudden professionalism only served to make Sam more tense.

"We have a question about exhibit number fourteen" she said through her clenched teeth.

"What is your question?" he asked nicely.

"What do you know about the Orb? How does it work?" said Rick.

"That's two questions," said the man.

"Well can you answer them?" said Sam.

"That's a third question...which do you want me to answer?" he said.

"Do you know how the Orb works?" said Sam, exasperated.

"Yes," he answered.

The team waited for further explanation, but none came.

"Tell us damn it" said Bernie, finally.

"I'm sorry, but that constitutes an interview, you will have to make an appointment with the receptionist once you have acquired your purple slip" he said.

"Jesus Christ!" shouted Jake.

"You're kidding!" cried Margaret.

"Somehow I doubt it," said Bernie, responding to Margaret.

"Let's just go, let's leave," said Rick.

"But they know how to use the Orb," said Ira.

"I doubt they'll tell us without a burnt orange slip with a pink fleck sparkle though...signed by the president in black ink" said Rick.

"You're probably right, let's get some lunch down stairs and we can look around, maybe there's some literature about it somewhere" said Sam.

They followed Margaret back down the stairs to the food court. She was beginning to feel like a tour guide, but she did know her way around the Museum better than any of the others. Sam had visited Cairo as a child, but she hardly remembered the Museum at all.

What she remembered most was to the Pyramids at the Giza Plateau just outside of town. Her family had taken her to see them and she was so excited that she had climbed a good fifty feet before she actually saw how high off the ground she was. She got scared and sat down on the limestone and cried until her parents came and got her. She felt so much better once they were with her. She would never forget sitting there on the side of Khufu's Great Pyramid with her mother and father. She smiled at the memory now as they waited in line at the food court.

"What are you so happy about?" asked Bernie, noticing her smile. He could see that her stress had suddenly melted away.

"I was just thinking about the Great Pyramids at Giza," she answered.

"I've always wanted to see those," said Rick.

"Well, what stopped you?" asked Margaret.

"Travel" he answered simply.

The others laughed and Rick shrugged his shoulders. After waiting in the long line they were finally able to make it up to the counter of one of the food venders. They placed their order together, to speed the process. The teen behind the counter rang up their order and told them the total. Sam handed over a wad of American Dollars.

"I'm sorry, I can't take these," he said.

"Oh...we have Egyptian currency" said Sam rummaging through her pockets.

"No, I mean, we can only accept food vouchers, it's 62 food vouchers." He said.

"Well where do we get food vouchers?" asked Sam.

The man pointed across the food court to yet another long line of people waiting in front of a counter.

"You've got to be kidding me," said Rick.

"So, I can purchase food vouchers with American money, right?" asked Sam.

"Yes" the man answered.

"Then why don't I just give the money to you and we can cut out the vouchers altogether" she said slowly, as she was painfully aware that she was dealing with a lesser human being.

"I'm sorry, we only accept food vouchers" he said again.

Sam sighed heavily, feeling very defeated by this new reality. Rick had pointed out that at least in this one, no one was trying to keep them prisoner. They laughed a little at that, but on the whole, their spirits were falling. Jake seemed to be getting very frustrated with all of this getting pushed around.

They purchased their food vouchers and again ordered their food. The total was, again, 62 vouchers. They had purchased a 75 credit voucher and paid with that. They were not given change. They ate quickly as they were all very hungry at that point. Bernie had left the table to throw away his garbage and had asked a lady by the trash cans if she knew what time it was. Her reply was that all questions were to be directed to the Customer Service Desk. When he sat back down, Ira obligingly told him that it was four in the afternoon.

After a brief bathroom break, they all met up again at the front doors of the Museum. Margaret had been clamoring for a smoke break, so they stood on the hot stone steps of the building while she and Jake sucked on their cigarettes. She stamped out the burning ember with the toe of her thick Timberland boot and commented on how her feet were killing her from all the standing in line. Sam enthusiastically agreed.

Margaret informed them that the Museum closed at nine in their native reality so they would need to find some information before then. They spent the next four hours searching the museum for literature on the Orb. Finally a fellow patron told them that all information about the exhibited items was available for purchase at the Information Desk.

The lines were shorter now that it was one hour before closing, so they were able to get to the desk by about eight fifteen in the evening. Once they were there, however, they were told that literature at the Information desk as well as all items in the gift shop could only be purchased using Museum Credits. They, of course, were available for purchase at yet another voucher desk, however, that desk was closed for the evening.

They were livid at this fresh news. They all complained and whined about how they would have to find a hotel for the night and try again in the morning. Jake was the only one who remained still. The others finally took notice of his stern, but distant expression.

"Jake, are you okay?" asked Bernie.

"NO!" he shouted, his eyes widening and twitching.

"Sir, I'll have to ask you to lower your voice" said the lady behind the Information counter.

"I will not lower my voice! You people have shoved us from one line to another all day and I'm fucking sick of it, you're worse than the Army for Christ's sake" he shouted at her.

"Sir...I'm sorry, but I'm going to have to get security over here if you don't pipe down" she said, picking up her desk phone and speaking softly to someone on the other end.

"Jake, you're gonna get us kicked out, man" said Bernie.

"This is just so stupid, I've...I've had enough, let's just leave, they probably don't know shit about the Orb anyway" Jake yelled, turning red in the face with anger.

"We've been told that they know how it works," said Ira.

"Yeah and we'll wait in line for ten years to find out that they don't know anything more than we do, so let's touch the Orb and leave!" he shouted.

"That's probably a good plan" said Sam motioning to the security force coming toward them.

They bolted for the Orb. Rick had tried to jump across the counter and grab some pamphlets as a last resort, but the lady behind the desk had whacked him on the head with her telephone receiver. This had put a painful end to his attempt at grand theft pamphlet. He ran after the others as they darted around the Museum. They made it to the glass outside the Orb's enclosure, but they were surrounded by security.

"On your knees!" shouted one of the guards holding a nightstick.

Jake pulled his sidearm out of its holster of his hip. Margaret swooned at such a manly display. The guards were shouting "He's got a gun!" repeatedly, and Sam just knew they were going to be put in jail for this.

"Drop the weapon and put your hands up" barked one guard.

"We require a yellow slip for you to arrest us" said Jake snidely.

"Yellow slip?" asked the guard, confused.

"I'm sorry all questions must be directed to the customer service desk" said Sam.

The guards' faces went red with anger and confusion, but before they could figure out what was going on, Jake had busted the glass with the base of his gun. Shards of glass rained down on the group as they hopped up on the display. The team ran to the Orb before the guards could give chase. The tinkling sound of the glass hitting the floor could still be heard as they touched the Orb and were again whisked off to another reality.

Chapter 23

The six found themselves in a small tiled room, where the device stood in the center of the room. There was a large mirror on one side of the room that showed the reflection of six travelers all cut to ribbons by the glass from the Museum. They were glad to find that at least the trip was a bit less painful this time, but perhaps it was just the adrenaline. Their heads rang and their bodies ached, but they hadn't passed out this time. Rick felt somewhat odd but had not yet thrown up. They commented that the trip was decidedly easier to bear this time. They had just enough time to ask themselves where they could possibly be before a door on one side of the small square room opened. Before them stood a man who was dressed in some kind of uniform, and was wearing a look of pure shock.

"Hallo," said Bernie, breaking the ice.

"Who are you, where have you come from?" the man demanded forcefully, despite the fact that his face was pale and his hands were shaking.

"It's okay, please don't be afraid" said Samantha calmly, sensing the man's apprehension.

"Are you...Ghosts?" he asked, swallowing loudly.

"Ghosts...no, we are living people" said Sam trying not to laugh.

"Why would you think that we're ghosts?" asked Rick.

"You appeared from thin air...I saw you, you appeared and you were touching the execution sphere" said the man, clearly terrified.

"Execution sphere!" said Sam, stepping forward toward the man. He backed away from them.

"We're not ghosts...really" said Bernie.

"Touch us if you like, you'll see that we are just as solid as you are" said Ira patting his arm to prove that it was solid.

"Touch you...yeah right, and die like the people who touch the sphere. No thank you!" he said, his voice trembling.

"Listen, no one dies when they touch the Orb, it takes them to an alternate dimension or some crap like that, but they don't die" said Jake.

"Baxter, please don't try to help," Rick said to Jake.

"Jeez, sorry" said Jake, offended.

"He's right though, no one dies when they touch the Orb" said Sam comfortingly to the man.

"Look here, I've worked here for ten years. I've seen more than my share of scum put to death here, and every single one of them vanished when they touched the sphere. So if you aren't ghosts...you must be criminals." The man's tone had changed to that of suspicion.

"Criminals! I beg your pardon!" exclaimed Margaret.

"What is this place?" asked Sam, hesitantly.

The man eyeballed them for a moment before answering. He seemed to be convincing himself that they weren't ghosts at all.

"This is a federal prison, and you're standing in the top security execution chamber. It's where the country's most heinous criminals are put to death" he said as though it was common knowledge.

"Well, that's not what the Orb does, and we are neither ghosts nor criminals" said Margaret.

The man, who was some kind of prison security officer it seemed, stepped forward cautiously and slowly extended his trembling hand. He reached out and tapped Sam's arm tentatively. He got a curious look on his face and again tapped her arm again. Seeming satisfied that she was solid, he touched her again, this time grabbing her. He spun her around so that he was holding her hands behind her back. Her friends moved forward, alarmed by his sudden actions.

"Because you are real, you must be criminals, I don't know how you got here, but you will be dealt with," he said, holding Sam tightly.

He backed up and hit an alarm on the wall outside the door to the tiny room. The air was pierced by a loud, pulsing noise that echoed through the rooms and halls of the facility. Though the team couldn't know the extent of the facility, they were able to hear that the alarm was being sounded over many locations, which indicated a building of considerable size.

"Let her go!" said Rick, with a severity that surprised even him.

Sam's eyes went wet with tears as the guard held her hostage with a hidden weapon that Sam could feel in the small of her back, though the others couldn't see it. Her eyes alone seemed to communicate this information to them, making them as much hostages as she was. A few short but tense minutes later, the room was filled with guards wearing the same uniform as the man with a death grip on Samantha. There was nothing the crew could do except comply with their captors.

The guards forced them through several grey, utilitarian looking hallways through the facility. The halls were dim and half lit at this time of night. They passed many doors, all of them with a tiny window near the top. They finally stopped in front of one of these doors. Inside was a small holding room that very much resembled the one that had held the Orb. This room was a little larger and held a metal table and chairs, but it too had a large mirror on one wall. Sam suspected that it was a two way mirror and that this was some sort of interrogation room.

The guards took Jake's sidearm and Margaret's lighter. They stripped them of all of their knives, pocket and utility alike. Strangely enough though, they allowed them to keep their watches and other personal items. This gave them hope. They all knew that they wouldn't be imprisoned with things like shoelaces or Sam's key necklace. They were told to be quiet and that an Interrogator would be with them shortly. The door was locked as the guards left the room.

"That's just great," said Jake sarcastically.

"This is a terrible situation," said Ira.

"Well, at least we know that if we're put to death, it only means that we'll touch the Orb" said Bernie.

"Yeah, except that if we don't all touch it at the same time, we probably won't end up in the same reality" Margaret pointed out.

"Out of the frying pan, into the fire" said Rick.

"Hang on, you might be onto something" said Ira.

"Excuse me?" said Sam, seeking clarification.

"When we touched the Orb the first time, we didn't know what it did and we ended up in a reality almost the same as ours. The second time we were all thinking about how the Orb works, and then we were in a place where the people supposedly know how the Orb works, but they wouldn't tell us; we were hassled at every turn. Then, we were all running from guards, and I personally was thinking that we might not live to get home, and we end up in a prison execution chamber" said Ira.

"What's your point?" asked Jake.

"I see!" said Margaret "You think the Orb reacts to our thoughts at the time that we touch it!"

"Precisely" said Ira proudly.

"I get it," said Sam, nodding.

"You guys are over my head again" said Jake.

"Look at the common elements...we were afraid of the guards there, and here we met scary guards. We were thinking that we might die; we end up in an execution chamber. We had been imprisoned back in Mali...now we're in a prison, we were being harassed and pushed around and here we are being hassled into jail" Ira said.

"Okay, I'm with you now. So all we need to do to get home is to think about getting home" said Jake.

"Maybe...maybe that's harder than it sounds though, because we were all hoping to get home last time we touched it too" said Rick.

"So...it doesn't react to our thoughts?" said Jake.

"Well, look at the first time" said Margaret "I was thinking about Maso being missing, and we ended up in a world where no one knows he exists."

"We were all thinking about the possibility of someone stealing the Orb, and that's exactly what we were accused of trying to do," said Sam.

"So then why were there two Ricks?" asked Jake.

"I don't know, maybe someone was thinking about me," said Rick jokingly.

"Maybe it draws from what we are thinking about and fills in the blanks" said Ira.

"Maybe, or maybe all of this is just theory. Everything we're talking about, difficulty, distrust, imprisonment, death, they are all common elements of life. Maybe we're seeing patterns where there aren't any" said Bernie.

"That's kind of morose isn't it Bernie?" said Sam.

"Maybe, but it's true. It is entirely logical to think that these depressing elements that are common everywhere in our reality are also common in other realities" he said.

"But then what about what Francois said. 'Getting home is entirely up to you'" Sam said, quoting what their friend had made a point of saying to them in English at their last meeting.

"I think he just meant that he didn't know; that it was up to us to figure it out" Bernie retorted.

"I think it's worth a shot though. Next time we touch the Orb, we should all attempt to clear our minds of everything except thoughts of home" said Ira.

"If we ever get out of here you mean" said Bernie kissing the cross he wore on a necklace around his neck.

"You know what's frightening though, it's obvious that no one's ever returned here using the Orb" said Sam.

"Who would want to?" said Rick laughing.

They agreed that they had a plan if they could get back to the Orb. After a long time of waiting, they became very tired. It had been a while since they last ate and it was getting to be very late at night. With nothing to do but wait for their so-called Interrogator, they each began to fall asleep one by one. Bernie had hunched over forward on the table and was sleeping with his head on his folded arms. Margaret and Jake had fallen asleep leaning back on their chairs with their arms dangling beside them. Ira was stretched out on the floor next to a wall snoring noisily. Only Sam and Rick clung to their wakeful state at this point.

Rick was leaning up against a wall in the corner of the room, while Sam attempted to copy Ira by stretching out on the floor. The room was brightly lit and stark. Its crisp appearance gave it an unfriendly feel, and the tile of the floor was less than inviting. It reminded Sam of a hospital, sterile and chilly. While the others had fallen asleep from exhaustion, Sam was feeling the effects of sleeplessness due to the harsh uncomfortable feel of the tiny room. She tossed and turned for a long time before giving up altogether and standing. She sighed heavily with frustration.

"Can't sleep?" whispered Rick from the corner of the room.

"Yeah sorry if I woke you" she said, turning to him.

"Nah, I can't sleep either," he said, opening one eye.

"You look pretty tired to me" whispered Sam with a slight giggle.

"Oh I'm tired alright, but I can't seem to fall asleep" Rick responded.

"Is it the floor or the temperature?" said Sam.

"It's mostly the light, but it is freezing in here," he said.

"I think sleep is out of the question for me," said Sam.

"Me too, wanna come sit down?" Rick said, patting the floor next to him. "Come on, pull up a tile". Sam smiled and crossed the room to his corner and sat down next to him. She sighed and shook her head discontentedly.

"Where is this interrogator person, it's been hours" she complained.

"They're probably waiting for morning," said Rick.

"Ugh. If we can just explain, then we can get out of here" she said.

"Hopefully," said Rick.

Sam put her hands on her head in frustration. It had occurred to her that they might not be believed about the true function of the Orb, but she was hoping that these were reasonable people. The folks in the last reality were hardly reasonable though. She felt like they were intelligent, but they were all so stuck on their own procedures that they couldn't feel sympathy or compassion. It certainly seemed that there was a lack of compassion here as well.

"What have I gotten us into?" she whispered.

"And so the point emerges," Rick said.

"No...that's not why I can't sleep, it's just...I feel like all this is my fault" she said.

"Yeah, I sensed that when you touched the Orb for the first time, that you knew exactly what would happen" he said.

"I had no idea what would happen!" she exclaimed in a loud whisper.

"Yep, you've had control over everything all along" he said.

"But I haven't!" she said.

"Really...then why do feel like everything is your fault?" he said.

Sam realized what he had been doing and sighed again. He was sweet for trying to cheer her up, but the truth was that she was their leader and she had led them to this end. She supposed that it was still a good sign if her team was trying to alleviate her guilt. She felt that if nothing else, this ordeal had made her a few friends.

"You're right, I can't beat myself up over it," she said.

"Feeling sleepy now?" he said.

"I told you...that's not why I can't sleep," she said.

The truth was, she was very tired, and her guilt was part of what had been keeping her awake. She talked with Rick for a little while before her eyes started to droop. It wasn't long before she drifted off into a heavy, dreamless sleep.

He was beginning to think of her as someone he could get used to sleeping next to. He respected her strength and her determination. She had done a very good job so far of remaining diplomatic and fair. He had first assessed her to be bossy and cruel, but he now saw that she was truly a good leader. She wasn't bossy at all; she made cool headed decisions and was fair about listening to her team and what they thought. He was pleased that they were becoming friends. He looked at her beautiful face as she slept leaning on the wall next to him. He put his arm around her comfortingly, and then he fell asleep,

It was early the next morning when the metal door to the interrogation room swung open with a loud bang that woke the crew from their much needed rest. Ira groaned as he got to his feet. Jake grabbed his neck in pain as he sat forward. His fingers were icy from the chill in the air, and he woke Margaret by placing them on the back of her neck. She screamed and slapped him playfully.

Sam was alarmed to find that her head had slumped over and was resting comfortably on Rick's chest. It was far more tender a position than she had intended her slumber to be. She sat up in a hurry hoping that no one had noticed how cozy she was next to him. His arm, that was draped casually around her as they slept, fell heavily to the tile floor as she jumped to her feet. Rick rubbed his eyes and also got to his feet. They crossed to the table and sat down in the uncomfortable metal chairs. Bernie lifted his head and yawned as he sat back in his chair. Ira sat down next to him.

"Hope you all slept well, we try to make you comfortable here" barked the man responsible for opening the door so loudly.

The six only groaned in response. He entered the room slamming the door shut behind him. He was accompanied by two large, goon looking guards who stood inside the door on either side. The sentries were expressionless as the Interrogator stared at the group of sleepy travelers. He walked up to one end of the metal table and glared suspiciously at each of them. His eyes were black and Sam thought they looked evil. He seemed to have no soul behind those eyes and it frightened her.

"Does someone wanna tell me what the hell is going on?" he said, scrutinizing them with his black, piercing eyes. "Speak up, how did you get here?" he shouted.

"You wouldn't believe us if we told you" said Bernie.

"Well why do you start by telling me then" he snapped.

"Look, we're not criminals, so let's just try and talk about this civilly, okay?" said Sam, trying to be diplomatic. "What is your name?"

"I make it a point not to get friendly with criminals" the man said curtly.

"Like I said, we're not criminals. My name is Sam" she said.

"Bill" he gave a brief false smile "and until your innocence is proven, you are criminals."

The man stared Sam in the eye with a resolve that terrified her. It was apparent that he was hell-bent on proving them to be wrong doers. A shock wave of fear trickled down her spine all the way to her trembling fingertips. The realization set in that she was not going to be able to reason with this monster of a man. Every cell in her body twitched with fright at the thought of this man. She was unsure if it was his overbearing manner or her feminine intuition, but she could feel that this man was the harbinger of some unknown horror.

"Bill, what is it exactly that you think we've done; what do you think we are guilty of?" said Bernie, calmly.

"I don't have a criminal mind so I probably couldn't imagine the atrocities that you've committed in your lifetime. I do know that you somehow broke into this facility, which is top security and that you were found by a security officer in the execution chamber. What I can't figure out is how you broke in, and what you intended to accomplish by tampering with the sphere." Bill glared at them.

"We didn't break in. We came from the Orb" said Margaret.

"Oh right, right. You came from the execution sphere. Sure" he said sarcastically.

"It's true! I mean do you know of any other way that we could have gotten in here?" said Ira.

Bill was silent, but seemed less than convinced. He waved his hand at one of the guards behind him, and the man turned and opened the door. Bill gave them one last long threatening glare before leaving the room. The guards filed out behind them and the door was again locked from the outside.

"This is such bullshit!" shouted Jake slamming his hand on the metal table.

"They're not serious about this criminal stuff. If they actually thought we were guilty of something then they would have separated us before interrogating us. They would have taken our fingerprints and asked if we have lawyers" said Ira, trying to be logical about the whole thing.

"The problem is, Ira, that's in our reality, that may not follow here" said Sam.

The group was quiet after that. Sam's words had really put into perspective the bad situation in which they now found themselves. They all felt somewhat hopeless as they sat quietly in the cold, stark room. There was no foreseeable avenue of escape and the painful truth was now upon them that they may never see the light of day again. Though no one wanted to admit it, it was on everyone's mind that they may well be put into a dark cell in this crazy reality and be forgotten.

Chapter 25

Around lunch time the crew was beginning to get very hungry. It had been more or less a day since their last meal. Bill had not yet returned to question them further. In fact, no one had entered the tiny interrogation room since his departure that morning. The team of six travelers was becoming restless and antsy. Tensions were running high in what had become their group cell. They sat in silence, each of them thinking about their unfortunate predicament. For no real reason, other than the stress of it all, they were beginning to get very angry.

"Can you stop doing that?" barked Ira, breaking the silence.

"What?" asked Margaret, defensively.

"That noise, stop it," he said.

"I'm not making a noise," she said.

"You're biting your nails and it's making a noise. Stop it" he said.

Margaret stopped biting her nails and the silence fell over the room again for a short while. Sam sighed out of boredom.

"Since we're on the subject of annoying habits, it wouldn't hurt my feelings if you could stop sighing like that" Margaret said to Sam. She responded simply by rolling her eyes.

"What the hell is that?" shouted Margaret.

"What?" said Sam.

"You just rolled your eyes at me. So, what, Ira here can tell me to stop biting my nails, but I can't ask you to stop sighing?" Margaret said antagonistically.

"I'm breathing, No you can't tell me not to breathe" said Sam.

"Oh lay off her already, Sam" said Jake barging into the conversation.

"Will you all just chill please" Rick chimed in.

"You know I could live without the sighing," said Bernie.

"I could live without the sighing and the biting," said Ira.

"I could live without the bickering" shouted Rick, not out of anger, but to be heard over the childish fuss of the others. They hushed themselves, realizing that they were just on edge because of their situation. Sam sat back in her chair and sighed. Margaret shot her a threatening look.

"I have to pee," said Sam.

Margaret lowered her eyes and mumbled "I have to pee too, but you don't hear me crying about it."

"I'm hardly crying, Margaret, I just happen to find it soothing to sigh occasionally, is that okay with you?" barked Sam leaning forward again. Margaret didn't answer, she only lifted both eyebrows in a surly manner.

"I have to pee too" whispered Ira.

"Nobody cares!" shouted Jake, feinting anger to be funny. A smile began to tickle their lips. Everyone started to chuckle a little, until they all exploded with laughter. They found themselves laughing to the point of tears. It wasn't that anything was really funny, and their situation was hardly a comical one, it was just the absurdity of it all. They were literally fighting about pee.

Suddenly the door swung open with a bang, the signature entrance of Bill the Interrogator. He glared at the giggling team with clear frustration.

"Urine trouble!" mocked Sam, and the team once again erupted with laughter.

"Laugh it up, but if you want to use the bathroom, now is your chance" said Bill, who was not amused by their revelry. The laughter tapered off and they got to their feet and headed for the doorway. Bill stepped aside.

"Girls this way, and guys over here" said Bill pointing.

The women followed a guard down the hall in one direction, while the men followed another guard the opposite way down the hall. The facility was more brightly lit then when they had been taken to the room originally. There were no windows though; no natural light at all. It was certainly a dreary place. The guard walking with Sam and Margaret wore no smile; no expression at all. It was as if he was trying to have no personality.

"This way" was all he said as he walked behind the ladies.

"Turn left here" he said when they approached an intersecting hallway. They did as they were told. The hall appeared to be exactly the same as the one before, and just as long.

"How big is this place?" asked Sam, noticing that there seemed to be no end to the halls. The guard did not answer.

"Bet you're great at parties" said Margaret sarcastically.

They walked in silence for a while longer through the massive establishment before reaching their destination. The guard had ordered them to stop in front of a door with a tiny window, like many of the doors they had passed on their tour. They stood as he unlocked the door and opened it. The room inside was a tiny cell. Like the rest of the facility's rooms that they had seen, this one was tiled in plain white but this room was in a poor state of repair. The white was dingy and old and some of the tiles were coming off of the walls. There was a small stainless steel toilet in one corner of the room that was dirty and smelled of over use. The room stank of the toilet and something else; something like fear. Sam felt very uneasy in this room that seemed heavy with loneliness.

"Is this the ladies room?" she asked the guard, as it was hardly what one would call a bathroom. It was tiny and it did have a toilet, but most bathrooms didn't lock from the outside.

"What is this?" she said.

"You're new home" he said as he shoved her inside. Margaret protested as he locked the door on her friend, but it had no effect. Sam's shouts from inside the room were silenced as the solid, soundproof door shut. Margaret struggled with the guard-turned-jailer but he forced her too into a cell only a little ways down the hall. Having locked the door, he walked away to return to his post. The hall was silent now with only the sound of the guard's footfalls as he abandoned them to their fate.

116

B ill made his way through the halls to his office. He knew his way around this place, though it had taken a while to learn. It was essentially set up like a grid, but there was very little on the walls of the halls to differentiate one from another. He had been an Interrogator there for nearly ten years now, so he knew exactly where he was going. He rounded a corner and headed directly for a door, like all the others, that had a tiny window. This door was different though, because it led to the outside. It was made to look like all the others on purpose, in case some brazen criminal got it into his or her head to try to bolt while in custody. Bill knew this door though, because it was the same one that he used every day to come to and from his place of work.

He used his key to open the door and exited the building. His car was parked just outside in the large parking lot. Being a respected Interrogator, he had been awarded a parking space close to the building so it was a short walk to his car. As usual on a Tuesday, he was at work until about two in the afternoon, which was the present time, and then he would leave to go to the strip club for the remainder of the afternoon and night. He had a simple routine, but it worked for him.

When he arrived at the strip club, he was met by a friend of his. The two greeted each other as usual and sat down at their corner table. Bill's friend, Marcus, asked him how his day at work had been. Marcus was also an Interrogator, and the two frequently swapped trade secrets and stories over beer. Bill relayed the tale of the strange folks who had inexplicably appeared in the execution chamber, claiming to be travelers.

"They claim to use the execution sphere to travel!" laughed Bill.

"Jeez, that's a new one" said Marcus

"Yeah, it gets better, while I was watching them in the holding room, they started talking about being from another reality" he said, taking a drink of his beer.

"Man, one time I had this crazy bitch who thought she was a dog. She kept licking herself. It was fucking funny" said Marcus as he hooted with laughter. He put his empty bottle aside and ordered two more beers for himself and his buddy.

"Yeah, it's weird, but they really seem to believe it" Bill said.

"No way, man" Marcus laughed.

"Yeah, but here's the kicker...we pumped H2 and T4 into the room. Not only were they telling the truth, but they were laughing" he said.

"Well T4 only works as a truth serum if they are lying, not if they're crazy and they actually believe what they say. That dog lady still thought she was a dog after four hours of breathing T4" said Marcus.

"Sure, but the H2 should have made them want to kill each other, and they were laughing! I mean the drug is designed to make people pissed off enough to confess, but they just sat there joking" said Bill, setting aside his empty beer and starting a fresh one.

"Yeah, that's pretty tough, but maybe they're just that crazy or something" Marcus said shrugging.

"I know it's weird, but I've seen the tape from the execution room, and they really did just appear from nowhere. I can't explain how they did it" Bill said, shaking his head.

"You're not telling me that you believe them are you! What's the first rule of being an Interrogator...never believe what the subject tells you!" said Marcus quoting the mantra of Interrogation.

"Of course not, but I really wanna know. It's pretty amazing, and I just want to know how they did it. But my orders were to stick them all in cells" he sighed.

"Well, if you really wanna know, you know where they'll be. You could always drop in on them sometime and Interrogate them" said Marcus.

"I guess I could," Bill sighed.

"Anyway, it might raise your spirits, man, cuz you look pretty down" Marcus added seeing that his friend was more somber than usual.

"So how's your work man?" Bill asked.

"I fucking broke my hand again last week" he said

"You get it fixed?" Bill asked.

"Yeah, cost me another five grand" Marcus groaned.

"Man, I'm telling you, if you're gonna use your fists, you gotta get better insurance" mocked Bill.

"Fuck you man, just cuz I Interrogate the old fashion way...not like you" Marcus said punching his fist into the upholstered bench where they were sitting.

"Whatever, there's absolutely nothing wrong with using Interrogation Aides, I find them quite effective" he teased back.

"Yeah, they used to laugh at me at the Academy, cuz my subjects always came out looking like raw hamburger" Marcus laughed.

"Man, I had one die on me last month, and she didn't have a bruise on her, it was beautiful except that she died without confessing" said Bill.

"Fuck, man that sucks, what killed her?" asked Marcus.

"They said it was the pain, but I think the bitch just gave up living" Bill responded with a shrug. He took another chug of beer and waved for the waitress.

"Mine usually go from blood loss or brain trauma" chortled Marcus, before ordering another couple of beers from the waitress.

They watched the show for a moment, before a new girl came out onto the stage. She started to dance, and Marcus gasped.

"Check it out man...she's one of old Wire's" Marcus exclaimed pointing to her missing hand. "That dude is fucking nuts, man, he uses piano wire to remove body parts from his subjects until they confess to their crimes. That's why they call him Wire" said Marcus with admiration.

"How does he get them to not bleed to death?" asked Bill, who was fascinated.

"Oh, he used to be a doctor, but he went to the Academy and became an Interrogator cuz the money's better," explained Marcus.

"Nice," responded Bill, thinking how handy a medical degree would be for Interrogation. "What was her crime anyway?" he asked.

"Hell, I don't remember...shoplifting or something" shrugged Marcus who was watching her intently. He found it somewhat erotic to watch the girl dance with only one hand. But then there weren't many jobs available to confessed criminals, so he guessed that she hadn't had many options. Still it was intriguing to see her swing around with one hand on the pole while she rubbed her body with the nub at the end of her other arm. It was by far one of the most tantalizing dances he had ever seen. He was hoping Bill was watching too and not about to monologue on the stupidity of criminals as he had a propensity to do after a few beers.

"Man, these people are fucking stupid, why don't they just confess their crimes and get released rather than getting Interrogated" Bill said shaking his head.

"Cuz then we'd be out of a job" Marcus said, laughing and hoping Bill wasn't about to go off on one of his rants.

"Our society is so forgiving and these people just abuse it. If you fuck up and do something wrong...If you steal or rape or kill...all you have to do is just confess and you're golden. But, no...these people want to insist on their innocence to the bitter end. I mean...just get absolved and get out, you know... so what if you lose a few of your basic rights...maybe you should have thought about that before becoming a criminal" Bill said.

Marcus rolled his eyes at his friend's diatribe.

"Damn, it makes me sick, these fucked up people who won't just confess. And then we have to keep them locked up for ages because the law says so. I think there should be a shorter sentencing period then fifteen years. It's so stupid. We keep them locked as if that's gonna make them confess, meanwhile their family sits back saying 'see, they're not guilty'. If they're not guilty, then someone would have confessed in those fifteen years that they were sitting in prison. Right. Then they'll go free instead of being put to death. Right?" Bill finished.

"Yeah..." said Marcus, put off of his good mood.

"Right?" said Bill again.

"Yeah, man Right...Fifteen years is too long to prove them innocent...Fuck, can we watch the lovely ladies take their clothes off now" he said, annoyed.

Bill shook his head at the sad fact that this pretty girl had to lose her hand because she wouldn't just confess to stealing. "She deserved it," he thought to himself.

Chapter 27

Jake Baxter was not used to confined spaces. He grew up in Oklahoma on what used to be a ranch. It wasn't used as such anymore, but his family still owned the large plot of land surrounded in trees. He had lots of room to run around and play, and plenty of old barns and stables to explore and tree house forts to fall out of. Getting hurt in this environment was unavoidable, but it made him into a strong kid. By high school he was tough and athletic. He made his name on the football team and toughened himself up even more.

He wanted so much to go to college, but his family was very poor. His father had died when he was in middle school, and his mother worked two jobs to support him and his two sisters. His father had been in the Army, so his older sisters had gone to college on the government's dime. Jake was never very smart, so he worked hard to earn himself a football scholarship, but it had been awarded to someone else instead.

He was forced to go into the Army as his father had. He was a model soldier, and even considered going career, but his dream of going to college was too important to him. He got out of the Army and moved back home and enrolled himself in a small University near his Mother's house on the ranch. He was in school for about a year before he received a letter informing him that he owed several thousand dollars in tuition. He had made some money in the Army and so he paid, but the real issue was that his father's benefits counted against his own. Between his year in college his two sisters, the benefits had run out and he couldn't afford to pay out of pocket.

He moved in with his mother and started to look for work. His mother resorted to picking up extra shifts to support herself and Jake, who had virtually no education and couldn't get a job in the economy of the day. She eventually died, the doctors told him it was cancer, but Jake knew that she was just tired; she had worked herself to death. After that, Jake borrowed some money and headed to the city where had gone from one security job to another. He eventually got the job on the Mali dig. It paid really well, and all he had to do was look after a bunch of scientists. He had assumed that it would be an easy assignment, but he was in it up to his eyeballs now. All he could do was laugh at the bizarre situation that he had been thrown into.

The wide open spaces of his childhood were a distant memory now. He could close his eyes and see the fields so clearly, but every time he opened them, he found that he was still locked in his three foot by six foot tiled cell. He sat on the cold floor, leaning up against the stainless steel toilet, staring through the tiny window in the door. From there, all he could see was the ceiling of the hall, but he could imagine that he was back home as a child in Oklahoma. This kept him from giving up.

He missed his companions. Even if that meant listening to Margaret prattle on about that scientific stuff that he didn't understand. She was really, very smart. She wasn't much to look at, he kind of thought she looked like a crazy cat lady or something, but he had gained the highest level of respect for her intellect. She was good company too, with a pleasant sense of humor and a kind nature. He loved her British accent as well. Jake thought it made her sound so proper even when she was kidding around. He would have given anything to be with her now.

Her company was unfortunately not the company he received, though. Instead, he was visited almost daily by Bill the Interrogator. The man would show up with two guards who would manhandle him down the hall to a larger room that looked like all the others, lined in dingy old white tile. This room had a chair though; a metal monstrosity with straps that was bolted to the floor in the center of the room. The grout between the tiles and around the bolts on the chair was stained brown with blood and shit from years of nefarious acts of torture.

The first time he was brought to this room, Bill had told him that it was up to him to stop the hell that he and his friends were being put through. He had explained that Jake need only to confess to how they managed to get in, and that they would be released. They would of course only have the rights of confessed criminals rather than the rights of regular citizens, but they would be free and forgiven. Jake was glad to hear it, and he happily divulged everything he knew about the Orb. Unfortunately, Bill didn't believe a word of it.

Now Jake received visits daily. Time after time he was taken by force to that awful room with the chair. Some days, he would suffer beatings, some days the torture was far worse. The Interrogator had shoved needles underneath all of his fingernails, run electrical currents of varying intensity through his eyelids, placed long plastic rods beside his eyeballs and used them to gauge his sinuses until blood came gushing from his nose and eyes, he had been shot repeatedly in the roof of his mouth with plastic pellets and on one occasion, he was bashed repeatedly in the nuts by a bag of sand and ball bearings.

He could no longer stand this treatment. He would have gladly put an end to it all, but what more could he do than tell the truth. He was more than ready to leave this place and the time had come. He had a plan; all he had to do was wait for the opportunity. He need only wait patiently for his next meal, which didn't actually come every day. Today, however, he was visited, though not by the guard who brought the food.

Bill strutted into the cell and his goons snatched up Jake and forced him down the hall to the torture chamber. They strapped him down in the uncomfortable metal chair and beat him for a while before Bill ordered them to stop.

"Have you decided to confess?" said Bill in a menacing tone.

"Fuck you!" was Jake's response, as had come to be routine.

"I'm beginning to get the feeling that you are never going to cooperate. Perhaps I should bring in one of your little bitch friends" said Bill. "The pretty one perhaps, she should be fun to Interrogate" he laughed maniacally.

Jake had learned that Interrogate was synonymous with torture. He cringed at the thought of what Bill might do to Samantha. He spit at Bill with hatred, his saliva and blood spattering over the man's face.

"Very well, I'll ask you again to confess," he said.

"I already told you everything I know" yelled Jake.

Bill was quiet. He seemed to be thinking of how he was going to torture Jake today.

"Hand me those crushers," Bill said to one of the guards.

The guard handed him a set of pincers that had rough spikes on top and bottom. Bill placed the device on one of Jake's pinky fingers and began to squeeze. He squeezed harder and harder as he asked Jake over and over to confess. The pain was excruciating, but Jake said nothing. He clenched his jaw and shook his head and screamed, but he said nothing to Bill. After hours of this Bill gave up for the day and took Jake back to his sad little cell. Jake's finger was useless, crushed and bleeding. He used a bit of his pant leg to wrap it up, but it was already purple and black from the abuse. He swallowed his pain and anger and thought only of his plan to escape.

He sat in his cell awaiting his meal. The guard finally came that day; he stuck his hand into the slot at the base of the door to retrieve the tin plate. Jake held his breath. This was it...this was the moment. Time seemed to slow as he waited for the guard to place the plate with food back through the slot in the door.

He watched as the flap covering the slat moved at the pressure of the guard pushing it. There before him was the plate of food, and attached was the guard's hand and wrist. Jake struck like a cobra, seizing the wrist and pulling as hard as he could. He was slightly encumbered by his swollen hand and pulverized pinky, but he was not going to give up. He put both feet on the door to brace himself and he pulled and twisted with all the strength he could muster. His strength was fueled by his anger, his hate and his pain. He heard a snap, but he kept on pulling and twisting the guards arm. He was only vaguely aware of the screaming, even when the bone snapped through the skin on the jailer's arm. Finally he stopped struggling. Jake wasn't sure if he had killed the guard or if he had just passed out from the pain. Either way, the man was incapacitated.

He pushed the arm back through the slot in the door and reached his own arms through. He began turning the body, shifting it around until he found what he was looking for. He grabbed the keys from the belt buckle and as a bonus he felt that the jailer was carrying a weapon of some sort. He grabbed that too and pulled his arms back through the door slot.

When he had been placed into the cell, he had thought it odd that the only items that the jailers took away from them were knives and Jake's side arm. He had thought to himself that one can pick a lock with near about anything if they know how. Upon being put inside he had found that there was no key hole on the inside of the cell; Jake would now have to unlock it from the outside. He managed to brace his legs in an almost split formation against the sides of the narrow cell. The tile was slippery at first, but the guard's blood solved that problem. It was starting to congeal on the cold floor inside the cell and he put some on his boots to make them just a little sticky. It gave him the edge he was looking for. He braced his legs on the walls and elevated himself to the height of the tiny window. Once there he was able to bust it out by bashing it repeatedly with the guard's weapon.

With the window mostly removed, he was able to reach through and get the keys into the lock. It took him a long time to get them into position and turn them, and his legs were giving way. Finally he managed to turn the key in the lock. His legs gave out before he could bring his arm back inside though. He cried out in pain as he dangled by his shoulder, but he eventually got his arm free and then he simply opened the door and walked out.

He pulled the guard's body into the cell that was formerly his unhappy home. As he locked the door, sealing the jailer inside, he gave a slight chuckle at the twist in fate. He used his shirt to clean up some of the blood in the hallway. He was thinking to himself how odd it was that no one had come to the sound of the guard's screaming. It was possible that whatever other guards might be around were just used to hearing screams of terror from the torture room just down the hall. Regardless of what the case might be, it was time for him to move, he would find his friends and they would leave this hell. He only hoped that they were still alive.

Chapter 28

Rick sat alone in his cell. The tin plate that had held the food they had brought him was empty and sitting by the slot in the door that it had come from. He stared at it spitefully. This room was a horrible little hole and that plate had more freedom then he did at the moment. He had never been envious of an inanimate object before, but that plate would get to leave this awful room, even just for a second while it was filled. That plate was a prince compared to him.

He sat huddled on the floor, cold and lonesome. His thoughts drifted to his friends who were no doubt in a similar hole as he. Mostly he thought of Samantha, who he had grown quite fond of, and he hoped that she was safe. All he could do was hope that his companions were alright. They had been led through so many halls; passed so many doors just like his. How many people must be imprisoned here? How many people's dreams turned to nightmares as they rot in a tiny cell like his? How long before he and his friends turned to dust in this hell? His head dropped into his hands as he began to weep.

The lights went out at eight that evening. There was only a dull glow from the half lit hallway. The dim light filtered through the tiny window in the door and gave an eerie hue to the tiny cell. Rick hardly thought it was possible for this room to look even drearier than it did before, but here was proof. He was mired in despair. With no bed in his little cell, Rick curled up on the tile and closed his eyes.

Days passed in this manner. Some days, food came through the slot in the door, and some days, there was none. He was beginning to feel very weak. It was not only the lack of food that pulled the strength from him, but the feel of this place also drained him of his energy. Each day that passed sapped more joy from his soul, and he feared that he would go insane. His only remaining joy was in imagining the last time they were all together. Even though it had been here in this horrible place, he was able to think brightly of the laughter they had all shared.

Night after night was filled with silence; a harrowing silence that began to eat away at Rick. One such night, as he contemplated his existence and likely death in this horrible cell, he became aware of a sound. It was the only sound he had heard in ages apart from the plate occasionally being filled. He listened as there was a slight knocking sound outside of his door. He glanced up, but saw no one. He thought perhaps he was already starting to go mad, but he could clearly hear keys in the lock. The door opened, and to Rick's surprise, it was Ira Philpot beckoning him to stand.

"Come on, we're getting out of here" he said in a whisper. It was strange, but Rick thought how odd it was to hear something after so long in cold silence. He was so happy to hear Ira's voice, especially when it brought words of escape.

"How...how did you get out?" asked Rick, the sound of his own voice as distant a memory as that of Ira's. He got to his feet and jumped from the cell into the hall with Ira and Jake.

"Jake busted out; I was the first one he found, then you. Now we gotta get the others and get out of here" Ira explained breathlessly.

Rick noted that Jake was bloody and clearly injured. He thought he'd better just follow for now rather than trying to get him to explain his horrific appearance. Rick's legs were stiff from lack of exercise, but he did his best to keep pace with the others as they jogged through the hallways. They hurried, checking room after room for their friends. Rick had asked how Jake managed to escape, but he was curtly told that it would be explained later.

They paused for a moment as they came to an intersection. Rick was glad to have the reprieve. He had been cooped up for so long that his muscles were already screaming from the short jog. Jake peered around the corner, hugging the wall. He made no noise; he only waved to indicate to the others to wait. Having been trained by the Army, Jake was more than adept at sneaking. He turned to Rick and Ira and mouthed the word "guard" so that they too would remain silent until the coast was clear.

A moment later, Jake peered out again. He slowly crept from their cover around the corner to the open hallway. It seemed to be clear now, so he motioned for the others to follow. He ran all the way to the next intersection and peered around as before. He turned to the two men he had in tow and whispered that the coast was clear for now, but that they would have to keep an eye out.

"I'll hold this end" he said "Rick, you take the other end while Ira checks these rooms. If you see a guard, don't yell, just quietly signal to me".

Jake was clearly in charge of this operation. He was not only the most qualified, but he had assumed the role of leader, and the others had followed. Rick and Ira did as they were told.

Rick stood watch on his end of the short section of hall. So far he had seen no one, but he kept a keen eye out for any sign of movement. He had never been in this sort of situation before and it made him feel strangely empowered. He was overcome by an emotion that was new to him. Somehow in this place he was able to find what could only be described as his inner badass. He had never stood against authority before, even when he was little and his father would beat him senseless, he had never been able to stand in opposition. Now, here in this awful place that he had come to despise, he was finally able to feel strong. He looked back at Jake who was still peering around his corner on the other end of the hallway. Rick thought how odd it was that everything about this man had been distasteful before, and now he was saving them all. Rick had hated Jake back in Mali, but now he had the greatest respect for him, and even found himself behaving like the soldier that he had previously despised.

Ira had finished checking all the windows of the many doors and had motioned for them to keep going. They made their way through the facility hallway after hallway. After many doors, many windows peered through and many hallways traversed, finally Ira called out to the two watchers.

"I got Bernie!" he said in a loud whisper. Jake and Rick joined him at a door. Ira fumbled the keys for a while. They managed to open the door and retrieve Bernie, who was hungry, but all in all, not too worse for wear. They gave him the brief explanation that they were busting out of this hell hole and that he would need to be quiet. Bernie nodded to indicate that he was with them.

"Let's get the girls and split" Bernie said in a whisper.

Now, with the two watchers and two to check the doors, the search of the facility was slightly quicker. There was once that they nearly ran into a problem when a guard was heading their way, but they were able to quietly hide around a corner while the officer passed them, apparently none the wiser.

They searched the facility, doing their best to keep track of where they were and where they had already been in this maze of a prison compound. Everything looked the same and several times they found themselves looking through windows that they had already checked. With no marking on the walls and no numbers on the doors, it was difficult to keep track. The only feature on any of the walls was the occasional red button resembling the one that the guard had hit days ago when they arrived. The team was careful not to brush against these buttons as they peeked around corners and slunk along the walls.

They searched in this fashion for what seemed like hours, though it had only been minutes. Their anxiety and fear of being caught seemed to make time slow to a crawl. Eventually they located Margaret. They opened the door and she raised her head wearily.

"Are you really here?" she whispered tearfully. She had clearly not been fed in far too long. Her tin plate was dry as a bone and there wasn't a scrap of food on it.

"We're here Margaret," said Bernie kindly.

"Jake...is that you?" she said faintly.

"She's delirious," said Bernie.

"Jake...you've come to rescue me so many times before...you can't be real this time either...be gone you wretched specter" she whimpered.

Jake stepped inside the cell and placed his hand on her shoulder. The others stood watch in the hallway.

"I'm here Margaret, it's me Jake, I'm here," he said sweetly to her.

"No...you're just a vision, you're not real, I'm going mad, I'm going mad!" she screamed.

The others immediately spread themselves out in the hallway as a response to her screams of terror.

"I'm not a vision! If I were just part of your imagination would I look like this" he said turning his face toward the open door, illuminating his pulverized face.

"Oh, Jake, What have they done to you!" Margaret gasped.

"Never mind that for now, let's just get out of here" he said, helping her up.

"Do you know where Sam is?" Rick asked her.

"She's bought more mules since her last visit" said Margaret reeling with weakness.

"It's no use" said Jake "she's passed out". He picked her up and carried her. A few rooms down they found Sam. They unlocked the door, but she remained asleep on the floor. Rick entered and the others remained in the hall. Rick placed his hand on her hair and stroked it gently, but she did not move. He shook her softly to attempt to wake her, but she still did not stir. He feared the worst. He looked up at Bernie who was poking his head in the door. Rick shook his head as though to say that Sam may not be escaping with them. His biggest fear was realized in that moment. He refused to think that there was any chance that she might be dead. Considering Margaret's condition, it was an unfortunate possibility. He died a little in that moment.

Suddenly she sprang to life taking him in a choke hold. She was clearly not dead, nor was she as weak as Margaret had been. Sam's strength of body and spirit was fully intact. She grunted as she choked Rick from behind. He was beginning to feel that he was in a dire situation until Bernie again poked his head in the doorway.

"Sam! You're okay! Thank God" he said grabbing the tiny cross he wore around his neck and kissing it.

"Bernie...Rick!" she said, seeing her old friend, and subsequently realizing that her attack had been on her ally, rather than an enemy.

"Oh Rick, I'm so sorry, are you okay?" she said embracing him now in compassion. He coughed for a moment then hugged her back.

"Glad you're okay" he coughed.

"I'm sorry, I thought you were them, I've been planning to escape for days" she explained.

"Jake beat you to it, he rescued us all" said Rick.

Samantha was surprised by this. She hadn't figured him for one to look out for anybody other than Jake Baxter. She thanked him, and then inquired about his face and Margaret's current condition. She, like the others had been, was told that he would tell his story some other time, perhaps when they weren't attempting to escape from a prison hell-hole.

Having found their last team member, the six set off to search the facility for the Orb room where they began this awful escapade. Rick and Sam took the lead as Jake's hands were full carrying Margaret's limp body through the halls. As they peered around a corner, there was a voice from behind them.

"Stop where you are!" shouted a security guard who was holding a weapon of dome kind.

Jake looked at Rick in the eyes and seemed to be motioning his eyes at something. Rick was confused for a moment. He could tell that Jake was trying to signal something, but he wasn't sure what. Jake made a face that clearly communicated his frustration. The security guard was slowly creeping toward the button on the wall that lay between him and the six jailbirds. Finally Rick saw what Jake had been trying so hard to motion his eyes at. In his back pocket was a weapon like that which the guard was pointing at them. Rick began to slowly move toward Jake to grab the weapon from his pocket.

"I said don't move" the guard yelled.

Rick was very close now. He was almost close enough to lunge and grab it. Sam, noticing what was about to happen, tapped Ira and Bernie to alert them of the impending action. Rick waited for a second until the guard's attention was again on the red button on the wall. He lunged, somewhat clumsily at the weapon in Jake's pocket. He grabbed it and pointed it at the guard.

"Back away from the alarm" Rick shouted to the guard.

The man glared at him. Rick shouted for him to drop his weapon, but the guard did not. Sam and the others dropped to the floor as Rick fired the weapon. An explosion crashed and the wall next to the guard crackled and burned at the force of this small, but powerful weapon. It looked rather like a TV remote, but was decidedly more powerful than it looked. The guard was stunned for a moment at the closeness of the blast, but, finding his situation a dire one, he lunged at the button on the wall. The guard's hand came slamming down on the button just as Rick fired a second blast. The guard was incinerated before them, and the alarm was sounding throughout the facility.

The team was in awe of the explosion of the man. No one more so than Rick, who had never killed so much as a fly in his life. Now it seemed that he was a murderer. He blinked heavily at the sight of the man's smoking and disjointed remains. He exhaled heavily at the gravity of what he'd done. His ears rang as his blood pressure jumped and adrenaline surged through his body.

Sam got to her feet hastily and grabbed his as he stared at the aftermath of his heroism. She pulled him from his frozen stare and shouted that it was time to go. They ran as fast as they could in the direction that they hoped the Orb room was located. They could hear shouting as officers came to arrest them. The halls pulsated with red flashing lights that only elevated the intensity of their plight.

The reunited team hastily made their way through the nightmarish facility in search for the Orb. They eventually located the room that had been referred to as the execution chamber. They entered and shut the door behind them.

"We have to be careful when we touch the orb" said Ira, "Remember, it might react to our thoughts".

"Well we all have a lot of bad thoughts right now, so what do you suggest we do" said Jake.

"We need to think of home," said Ira.

"Yeah, but we're all thinking about the shit we just went through, it's on our minds, what if that has an effect on the device" said Sam.

"We don't want to end up in a place that's even worse than this," said Jake.

"Concentrate on home, think about it as hard as you can," said Ira.

"If you start to think something...negative, just think of something happy instead" said Bernie.

"Fine, let's just do this before we get put back in our cells" said Rick holding the weapon on the door in case the guards busted in on them.

They all took a deep breath. Bernie put his hand on Jake's shoulder as his hands were full holding Margaret. The rest of them joined hands as Sam reached out and touched the Orb.

Chapter 29

The team found themselves in a nice sort of place this time. It was certainly not home, but it was beautiful. They were surrounded by plants and flowers. The air was warm and sweet and the songs of birds filled the background. Anyone might have called such a place paradise. There were broad leaves wet with dew that brushed their arms as they stood around the Orb. The many colors of this rainforest were a welcome change from the colorless and drab prison. The vibrant flora reflected off the Orb, making it seem almost alive.

"Well, this isn't home" said Jake laying Margaret down on the soft bed of the forest floor.

"It's the nicest place we've seen so far," said Sam.

"I bet we can find some food here, maybe we can use this weapon to kill some kind of animal or something" said Rick.

"Sure, if you want to pulverize it completely" said Sam, sarcastically.

"We should probably just use that for defense" said Bernie.

"We should at the very least look for fruit or edible plants" said Rick.

"We shouldn't wander too far from the Orb though" said Ira.

"Okay, it's day break now, we should spend the day setting up a campsite," said Sam.

"What...No...we should eat and be on our way," said Ira.

"We have no idea where we'll end up next; we should camp here and recuperate before we use the Orb again" said Sam.

"We'll get home if we concentrate on home" argued Ira.

"I don't think that's how it works, I mean we all concentrated on home this time and we ended up here" Rick said, raising his voice.

"Yeah, but we didn't account for Margaret being knocked out, she could be thinking anything" said Ira.

"Stop it, both of you!" cried Sam. "We don't know why we ended up here, but it is a good idea to rest up and get our strength up before we try again".

Ira seemed to want to protest further. He was sure that his theory about the Orb was right, but he couldn't prove it.

"There's gotta be plenty of food and fresh water, and as far as we know, the Orb sends us to random places" Sam said.

"Fine" said Ira, throwing his hands up in frustration.

Sam convinced Ira to help find some firewood while She, Rick and Bernie went into the woods to search for food. Jake stayed by the Orb to look after Margaret who was still unconscious. Sam held the weapon in case they stumbled on some wild animal. She was determined to protect her team here as she had not been able to in the last reality. They were all still very wound up from their daring escape from the prison, and as pleasant as their new surroundings were, the jungle was far from a safe place to be.

Sam kept a keen eye out as they marched through the wet plants. She jumped at nearly every sound that came from the brush. She was hardly afraid; she was just very on edge as they journeyed through the unknown. As they traversed the jungle forest, it began to rain heavily. They flung their heads back and stuck their tongues out to catch the dripping water. They laughed at the absurdity of trying to drink water from the sky. It was the first time in many days that any of them had laughed.

It wasn't long before Sam, Bernie and Rick came upon trees that were filled with some kind of fruit. The trees were large and had little oval leaves and the fruit was round and had a thick green rind.

"Do you think it's edible?" asked Rick.

"Margaret would know" answered Sam.

"Funny isn't it?" huffed Bernie "We all had to sit through that boring 'Survival in the Sahara' seminar before going to Mali, and here we are lost in a damn rainforest".

"The principles stand though" said Sam.

"You mean we should eat bugs and dig for water?" said Rick, jokingly.

"I mean that water, food and shelter are still our top priorities, just like the seminar said; nothing's different but the venue" she said.

"Actually those things should be easier to come by here," said Rick.

"Well let's get some of these fruits back to camp, and then we can look for water" said Bernie.

They marched back through the jungle toward the Orb. Ira had been searching the immediate area for fallen trees or small saplings that they could use for a campfire. He had a small pile so far and was still adding to it. He pointed out that all the wood was wet and thus would be very difficult to light.

"How's the search for food?" he asked as the three returned.

"We found these, but we don't know if they are edible or not" said Bernie.

"We're going to look for some water to drink," said Sam.

"How is she?" asked Rick, referring to Margaret.

"She's beginning to come around" said Jake as he patted her gently on the cheek.

"She needs water, she's very dehydrated," said Ira.

"I was able to get some of that rain into her mouth, but she'll need more than that" said Jake.

"Okay, let's go find some" and with that Sam and Rick disappeared through the brush.

Sam instructed the others to squeeze the juice from the fruit to keep Margaret hydrated. She showed them how to collect water droplets from the broad leaves of the jungle and to collect them up together for drinking water. She had also told them to keep her as warm and dry as possible, the last thing they needed was for her to contract some disease because of her weakened state. With her immune system so low, they would really need to keep an eye on her. On top of that,

Jake was injured as well, and Sam knew that jungles are notorious for being home to parasites and bacteria. Whatever water they might find would probably be teeming with sickness. They would just have to do their best for now and hope that they could get to a doctor soon.

Rick and Sam marched their way through the thick jungle bush towards the fruit trees that had been found earlier. Bernie had stayed behind with the others to assist them with nursing Margaret back to health. It was getting close to midday and the bugs were in full attack mode.

"I just hope these mosquitoes aren't carrying malaria or something," said Sam.

"You sound like Maso," laughed Rick.

"I hope he's okay" said Sam with a far away stare.

"He could be anywhere; he could even be rotting in that prison" Rick said.

"There's a happy thought," said Sam, cringing.

They climbed through the forest until they had arrived at the fruit trees. From there they followed a line of trees to a rocky outcropping that overlooked a stream about twenty feet below them. The water appeared muddy, but it was moving fast, so Sam reasoned that parasites and bacteria might not be as much of a concern.

"How do we get down to it?" said Rick.

"We'll have to find a path around," said Sam.

The drop was too much to try and jump, especially since they had no idea how deep the water was or how strong the current might be. There was also the concern of what creatures might be lurking beneath the rippling surface.

They hiked along the ridge as far as they could. The trees were thick and the jungle was dense. They finally made it to a low point in the ridge line where they could hop down to a small bank below. From there, they could fill the only vessels they had that would actually hold water; Margaret's shoes. She was the only one who wasn't walking around in this jungle habitat, so she had been made to relinquish her footwear for the good of the team. Unfortunately this meant that their drinking water would taste something like sock, but it was better than no water at all.

Rick helped Sam drop down the five feet or so to the bank. He remained up top in order to help her back up again. She bent down to the river's edge and gave the shoes a healthy rinsing before trying to fill them. Using Rick's shirt, she filtered the water of its mud and grime. She got one filled and handed it back to Rick. She bent back down to fill the other one, but as she leaned over the water, a startled snake leapt from the bushes beside her. She dropped the shoe into the water and the current swept it away. The snake had not bothered her in any way other than the initial scare it gave her, but the unfortunate result was that Margaret's left boot was long gone down the river.

Rick helped her back up onto the ridge. His shirt was filthy with leaves and mud from the river water. Sam apologized to him for the state of it.

"Better on my shirt than in our drinking water," he said.

He shook the shirt and slung it around to attempt to rid it of its muck. Sam caught herself looking at his bare chest as he wrung out his soaked tee. He was surprisingly muscular for a lab geek, and Sam found herself a little turned on by his naked upper body. She looked away to keep herself from gazing at him lustfully. He put his shirt back on and they carried the water filled boot back to camp.

They showed up with a shoe full of water and a branch of berries that they ran across on the way back. Margaret was sitting up now and was munching on one of the fruits.

"Glad to see you're awake" said Sam, smiling at her.

"I feel bloody awful," she said.

"Well, have some water, and eat some berries, and hopefully we can get a fire going for you" said Rick.

"Where is my boot?" she said, alarmed, but still weak.

"Sorry" said Sam squinting sheepishly.

"You lost it!" said Margaret.

"She got scared by a little lizard and threw it into the river" laughed Rick.

"It was a snake and it was huge!" cried Sam "and I didn't throw it".

Rick rolled his eyes, teasing her. She punched him playfully in the arm in return for his ragging on her.

They used the hollowed out rinds of the fruit as cups and passed around water to the team. Sam passed the branch of red berries to Ira who ate a few and passed it on to Margaret.

"Where did you get these?" she cried.

"From the corner store" Sam said sarcastically.

"Very funny, but these are poisonous" Margaret cried.

Ira started coughing and spitting trying to rid himself of the berries he's just finished chewing.

"You let me eat poison, you made me drink stinky foot water...Are you trying to kill me!" he shouted.

"Relax, you only ate a few, you'll probably just get a stomach ache. And my feet smell like roses, I'll have you know" Margaret said, her humor coming back.

They ate and rested for a while longer before they decided to try and light a campfire. They had great difficulty getting the wet jungle vines to catch on fire. Rubbing the sticks together seemed to be a futile endeavor, so they had resorted to knocking rocks together to create sparks.

"It still might be too wet to burn," Sam pointed out.

"We'll need some sort of catalyst, something to get it started so the green wood can dry out" said Rick.

"Paper would be perfect, but we don't have any paper," said Sam.

"Funny...the things you take for granted," said Rick.

Sam was quiet. She was thinking seriously on his words. There were so many things that she had either taken for granted or thought of as valueless that she had a brand new perspective on now. Things like toilet paper, and central heat and freedom. She even thought of some *people* as having no value, but back in that prison, she would have killed for a friend, any friend. Now she was surrounded by friends and all they seemed able to do was bicker and argue about the Orb.

Rick looked at Sam for a moment, seeing her expression had changed. Her face was so pensive, so introspective. He suggested that they look around in the forest for some kind of kindling for the fire. Everyone agreed, but his real motive was to make Sam feel useful. She had the same stare now as she had worn in the prison; an expression that betrayed her guilt at having led her team on such a bizarre expedition.

Once they were away from the others, he asked her if she was okay. She began to cry a little, despite herself. He hugged her sweetly, and she hugged him back. They held each other for a second then they released their embrace. As they separated, their eyes met for an instant; in that moment, all he wanted was to kiss her, and for one glorious second, he thought maybe she wanted to kiss him back. As it happened he didn't kiss her and she turned away and the moment was over.

The rest of the hike was quiet. The only thing either of them said was the occasional warning about a patch of briars or a slippery rock. Eventually they were able to find some tender for the fire in the form of a hairy bark that grew on one of the trees they found. They grabbed as much as they could carry and went back to camp to build their fire.

"Feeling better?" asked Rick.

"Thank you," she said.

Rick felt accomplished. She was a fine leader; she just needed someone to remind her of that every now and then. They once again tried to light the fire, but their efforts were as futile now as they had been before. Sam pulled some money out of her wallet. It was dry compared to the bark and the leaves, but it still wouldn't light. The failure was disheartening to them all. Finally, Sam offered a bit of her hair as kindling. She used a rock to shred bits of hair from her head and placed it on the rocks where their fire was to be. A few sparks later, they were able to light the hair and the money. The tiny blaze eventually caught the bark and the sticks in turn. Before they knew it, they had a fully burning campfire. Their accomplishment was a small one, but it gave them a sense of hope that they had not felt in a long time.

The six sat around the fire as the sun began to sink in the open sky. Ira was curled up in pain for most of the afternoon due to the berries, but he seemed to be fine now. The belly ache was minor, and the large amount of fruit he had consumed had moved the berries through his system quickly. They all now engaged in light conversation over the remainder of the fruit.

"I don't remember much" Margaret said "How long were we in that awful place?"

"We were there for days," said Sam.

"There's no telling how long you went without food" said Bernie.

"I know they sure didn't feed me everyday" said Rick picking up a piece of fruit and munching on it.

"Jake saved us all" said Bernie, patting him on the shoulder.

They all chimed in, thanking him repeatedly for saving them all. They asked again how he managed to get out of his cell.

"You must have been very brave," said Margaret.

"It wasn't bravery that got me out. It was anger and hate" he said gravely. "It was a dark, ugly side of me that got us all out of there, a side of me I never want to see again" he added.

The team was silent. They were able to tell by both his tone and the evidence of blood and violence on his clothes and on his body that it was something that was never to be mentioned again. Respectively, they changed the subject of conversation to something a bit lighter in nature. They talked of home and how they missed things like television and coffee.

"I'd kill for a nice hot Café Latte right now" said Sam.

"Blueberry pie with vanilla ice cream" said Margaret rubbing her stomach.

"We could probably use a doctor, as long as you're wishing for things" said Ira.

"Oh...there's this restaurant in my hometown that serves the best blueberry pie in our reality," said Jake, his mood lightening.

"Maybe you can take me there sometime," Margaret said flirtatiously.

Bernie began laughing hysterically at this. Margaret's face turned red and her expression read that she was greatly offended.

"What's so funny?" asked Sam.

"Well, Margaret was a bit delirious when we rescued her" said Rick, stifling a smile.

"I had gone a long time without food" said Margaret "So whatever I said was ridiculous I'm sure"

"So?" asked Sam.

"She was talking about how Jake was her big, strong hero and he had come to rescue her!" said Bernie in a false feminine voice.

"I most certainly was not!" cried Margaret.

"Oh yes you were, you were all about Jake being your knight in shining armor" said Rick, laughing.

"Well...I..." stammered Margaret, turning even more red.

"You thought he was part of your imagination, because you had imagined him rescuing you so many times before" Bernie mocked her.

"I didn't," she gasped.

"Oh yes you did...but that's okay, because I did rescue you" said Jake looking sweetly into her eyes. Then to everyone's surprise, Jake blushed.

The team hooted, half teasing the romantic gaze that the two now shared. They then pointed their blushing faces downward, embarrassed by the public nature of their flirting. They made a point of sitting very close to one another after that though. The others pretended to not notice, though their affection was quite obvious. They talked for a while until they all grew very tired. One by one they fell asleep under the black, starry sky.

Chapter 30

S am awoke to find that the sun had not yet risen in the sky above the tropical paradise. She was happy to find that it had not all been a dream, a delusion of her mind. She had been so miserable in that prison cell that she feared all of this might have been a creation of her imagination. Yet here she was, in dark jungle beauty with the finest and bravest friends that anyone could ask for.

She stretched her arms out in front of her and yawned. She was stiff and damp from sleeping on the wet jungle moss. She had no idea what time it was. Rick was wearing a watch though, so she leaned toward him as silently as she could to try and take a glimpse. She gently turned his wrist to be able to view the face of his watch. It read five o'clock in the morning. Rick's eyes opened as she leaned toward him.

"What time is it?" he said.

Sam told him the time and apologized for waking him. He explained that she hadn't, that he had been half awake for a while.

"Do you think we should wake the others?" she whispered.

"Better let them sleep for a while," he said, sitting up and rubbing his damp chilly arms.

They laughed softly as they watched the others sleep. The fire had gone out and the rest of the team was curled up as they slumbered. Margaret and Jake were very cozy spooning up together. Ira was snoring as he rested in a position that reminded Sam of her cat. Bernie was stretched out on his back with his protruding belly sticking up toward the canopy above them.

"Funny that they should get together" said Rick referring to Jake and Margaret.

"Why do you say that?" asked Sam.

"Well, he didn't strike me as the type to see past a woman's looks" he said simply.

"Yeah, I thought he was kind of an asshole, and I can only think what he thought of me when we first met" she said remembering their first meeting.

"I thought you were a bitch" Rick volunteered.

"Yeah I know, you told me, remember" she said smiling.

"But I don't think that now," he said.

"Good," Sam said nodding, decisively "I wouldn't want you to think I was a bitch".

"Really? I didn't think you cared what anyone thought of you" he chuckled.

"I care what you think" she said despite herself.

He wanted to be nearer her so he scooted closer, but once he was, he was only able to fidget nervously with his hands. Even after all that they had been through, he was still nervous around a pretty girl, especially one he liked. Sam turned her head and looked at him. For a moment he wasn't sure why. The thought crossed his mind that she might like him too. She was certainly looking hard at his face right now. Was it possible that she wanted to kiss him as he had wanted earlier?

"Hold still" she whispered. He did as he was told. Sam reached out her hand and touched his face. Rick felt goosebumps surge over his skin. He looked into her eyes, but they weren't gazing back into his. She seemed to be focused on his cheek. She drew back and in her fingers she held a beetle. She smiled at him as she threw it into the scrub. Rick's expression must have read great disappointment.

"You didn't want to keep it did you?" she said, jokingly.

"No," Rick said laughing. "Thanks for debugging me".

"Anytime" she said with a wink.

There she was gazing at him in the moonlight, and telling him she cared what he thought and touching his face. He was unsure if this was an overture of some romantic feeling or if she was simply reacting to the dire situation that had brought them all together as friends. Regardless of her intentions, Rick was captivated by her at that moment. Unable to help himself, he leaned toward her; a prelude to a passionate kiss. To his happy surprise, he found that she was also leaning toward him. He was so close to her beautiful lips that he could almost taste her, but their romantic interlude came to an abrupt halt as an ear piercing screech pierced the air. They quickly turned to find that Bernie was not only awake, but he was jumping around squealing like a little girl.

"Bernie! What's..." Sam began.

"Where is it...it was on me...where is it?" he shouted.

By now everyone in camp was awake. They all seemed to be trying to figure out who was being murdered. Bernie explained, not calmly that there had been a tarantula on him when he woke up. Bernie was terrified of all arachnids, spiders and scorpions especially.

"Oh, you mean this little fellow" said Margaret, picking up the huge spider.

"Put that thing down, are you insane" cried Bernie.

"Well it's hardly going to take my arm off now is it?" she said.

"I used to have one as a child," said Ira.

"Me too" she said smiling "his name was Big Ben".

"Mine's name was Harry...because he was hairy," said Ira in a rare display of humor.

Everyone giggled except for Bernie, who was truly horrified that everyone was treating this creature like a pet when in his opinion it was vermin. They let the tarantula go, and, as everyone was now awake, they began to discuss their next move.

After much discussion, they decided to eat and get some more water before moving on. Margaret requested that someone other than Sam retrieve the water. The thought of losing her other boot to the river was not ideal. Jake volunteered for the task and marched off with the boot through the jungle led by Rick.

Ira said he was going to look for more fruit. Bernie volunteered to search for fruit as well in a direction they hadn't yet explored. Margaret, being shoeless and still very weak stayed with Sam at the campsite. Sam was less than thrilled at the thought of everyone splitting up in this unknown environment. She asked them all to hurry back.

Sam sat with Margaret talking about her newfound friendliness with Jake. They giggled girlishly and she almost felt as though she was at a slumber party rather than in the middle of a jungle forest. Thinking that there was a better use of her time, she set out to find some wood. Having collected a few long, sturdy sticks, she began sharpening them into spears in the hopes of hunting for food. Eventually, she left Margaret by the Orb and wandered into the wilderness.

She crept through the woods, silent as a mouse, but as ready to strike as a coiled snake. She listened for any sounds that might give away the position of a rabbit or a squirrel. The loud calls of birds were all around her, but she knew better than to try and spear a macaw or a parrot. Strangely enough, a dead macaw landed at her feet. It seemed to have fallen right out of the sky and hit the ground with a thunk about five feet in front of her.

She shook her head in disbelief of the odd fortune she had happened upon. She picked up the unfortunate bird and wondered if it was even safe to eat. It might not even be safe to touch, she thought, if it had simply fallen from the sky. It could be sick or diseased. She considered tossing it away, but as she reared back to hurl it into the jungle, Rick jumped from the bushes behind her.

"Don't!" he cried. Sam turned, alarmed by his sudden appearance.

"It took me forever to actually hit one," he said.

"Hit one?" Sam repeated, confused.

"Yeah, I thought we'd have a little chicken for dinner" he chuckled.

"You killed it?" she said, still puzzled.

"Yeah, I built this slingshot using a stick and a weird sort of stretchy vine that I found. I was trying to use it to knock some fruit out of the higher branches, but the fruit kept exploding whenever I hit it. So, I decided to use it to hunt instead" he said smiling.

"Jeez, I thought it just fell from the sky, I was gonna throw it away because I thought it was ill or something" Sam explained, laughing. Rick laughed too at her foolishness.

"Did you and Jake get some water?" she asked.

"Yeah, he's with Margaret back at camp" he said "she told me what direction you went off in and I was able to pick up your trail" he said.

"Well, since you're such a woodsman, why don't you get us some more birds?" Sam said. Rick smiled; that was perhaps the first time anyone had ever referred to him as a woodsman, which was a manly profession. He had never been particularly manly. It was odd, but having shot the guard back in the prison and the bird just now made him feel angry. He had always had a great respect for life. He still did, but he now had an even greater respect for living creatures. He had killed only in self defense and out of the need for food. His motives for killing may have been noble, but Rick still felt a sadness at having taken lives. He felt it was more of a duty to his companions to kill now, and he was only hunting to feed his friends. He stalked through the woods shooting rocks at birds while Sam collected ammo for him from the ground.

Chapter 31

Ira wandered through the jungle forest of this strange and beautiful place. He considered thoughtfully the factors that might have made this reality so. He thought it strange that they had found no signs of indigenous human life, but then it was a jungle after all. The Orb in the last reality had presumably been moved to its location within the prison, but the likelihood of the Orb having been placed here was small. If it had been moved from its location in Mali to this jungle paradise, then they should have seen evidence of the people who moved it. As there was no such evidence, then they must be in Africa.

The thought about all the factors that would be involved in the possibility of Mali being a lush tropical rainforest versus its actual desert condition in the reality he knew. It must have been something so far back in the creation of the Earth that made this reality so vastly different than his. There was no way to account for the many circumstances that might differ between these two worlds.

He laughed a little at himself. He really thought of this place as another world. It was the same world he knew, just under a different set of circumstances. It was conceivable that in the multitude of possibilities, there may exist a reality where the sky is purple and it rains applesauce. Truly, anything was possible with the right set of factors in place. He considered this at length as he paced through the plant life of this wondrous jungle.

As he walked, he became aware of a rustling in the bushes around him. He froze in fear. There was no telling what sort of fauna might exist here. Saber tooth cats jumped to mind first, though they were never thought to be a jungle dwelling animal. Still his imagination was running wild with fright. He listened as a large creature quietly moved through the brush toward his position. He could almost see the image of a tiger or a panther ravaging his body with sharp claws and pointed teeth. He gulped loudly. His instinct was to run, but his stifling fear prevented it. He stood locked in place as his certain death crept nearer.

Suddenly the brush broke in front of him. He sighed heavily as Bernie came through the bushes.

"Oh, Hallo Ira," he said casually.

"Bernie! You scared the shit out of me, I thought you were some kind of creature" said Ira, breathing heavily.

"I may be an animal in the sac, but here, I'm just Bernie" he replied, laughing.

"Thanks for that image," said Ira, a little disturbed.

"Hey, you gotta come see this, there's this great overlook and you can see the whole valley" Bernie said excitedly.

They marched through the forest for a while. Ira's sleeve became snagged on a briar and he was somewhat stuck for a moment. Bernie was able to free him by using a set of keys he produced from his pocket. Once liberated from the spiny branches, they continued along their path with Bernie leading the way. Ira followed Bernie through the jungle to a rocky section of earth that looked out over a massive valley full of trees and plants. The sky above them was bright blue and white and seemed to breathe peacefully as they took in the incredible scenery.

"Wow!" Ira exclaimed.

"Is this something or what!" said Bernie smiling.

"This is something...it's amazing" gasped Ira.

The two surveyed the terrain for a moment. They were silent as they gazed out over the lush valley. The tree tops were small from this rocky overlook, and it was impossible to tell how high up they were or how large the valley really was. It was clear that the area was huge though. The men were dwarfed by the magnitude of the landscape.

"Do you know what I see here?" said Ira after a while.

Bernie shrugged and said "Greenery?"

"I see beauty and life" said Ira, "My father could look at this and all he would see is money. It's because of people like Steve Philpot that rainforests are chopped down in our reality. It's all about money to him." Ira frowned for an instant, but the beauty of the landscape soon turned his face back into a placid, calm expression.

"Unfortunately, money is what makes the world go round" said Bernie.

"It is unfortunate," agreed Ira.

The two men sat down on the rock out cropping and gazed out at the largest rainforest that any living human would ever see.

Chapter 32

Having reconvened back at the camp, the six made another small fire to cook the bird. The tiny fire smoked and snapped as they roasted the single macaw over the flames. Rick had pulled all its feathers off and Jake had gutted it with his bare hands while Sam had used water collected from leaves to rinse it of the blood and remaining down. Bernie had smeared it with the juice of one of the fruits they had found to give it flavor. What they now had was a jungle gourmet meal of roast macaw and nameless fruit. It was a simple meal, but any one of them would have called it the best lunch ever. The work and anticipation that had gone toward this meager appetizer was enough spice to cause this meal to be the best one any of them could remember.

"No offence to Francois" said Bernie with his mouth full of macaw, "but this is incredible".

"I just wish we could have gotten more than one," said Rick.

"Oh, no, you have done so much for us Rick, thank you" said Margaret.

"I think we might have been able to get a bagger or something if it weren't for the fact that we haven't showered in over a week" said Sam.

"You're probably right, any land dwelling critter could have smelled you a mile away" said Jake, laughing.

"Hey!" said Sam, slightly offended.

"You don't smell so hot yourself there Jake" Rick said, giving a sideways smile.

"Well, the bird is good, no matter how we smell," said Bernie.

They ate with enthusiasm, and decided to leave shortly thereafter, which was only just after noon.

They began by attempting to pinpoint what exactly had brought them to this place. As nice as it was, they had been operating under the assumption that if they all thought of home, they would get there.

"I just don't think it works like that," said Sam.

"It's too easy, you can't just wish to go home and poof, you're there" said Jake.

"But it seems like the Orb has been reacting to our thoughts" insisted Ira.

"Okay, raise your hand if you were thinking of a jungle when we broke out of prison" said Sam sarcastically.

"I was just trying to think happy thoughts," said Bernie.

"I have to admit that the wide open spaces of my childhood home were on my mind" said Jake.

"Okay, that might explain the natural setting" said Ira "What about you two" he said to Rick and Samantha.

"I was thinking about food" said Rick "and home of course" he added.

"I was trying to focus on home, but it did creep into my mind how much I longed to see the outdoors" Sam said, the others agreed that it was on their mind that they longed to see the sky and trees.

"Well I suppose that covers it" said Ira "and there's no telling what was on Margaret's mind while she was asleep".

"Ooh, actually, I do recall dreaming of food...and Jake" she said smiling.

"Well I guess that just about explains it," Rick said, ironically.

"I still say that the device draws on our thoughts" insisted Ira.

"Either it's completely random, or it draws on random thoughts" said Sam.

"But if it's that random, how will we ever get home?" asked Bernie.

"It may be that we just don't have the brain power to focus hard enough to get home" said Rick.

"We should keep trying though," said Ira.

"Oh I do agree" said Margaret. The others chimed in that it was the best course of action for now.

"There's nothing to do now but try again, then" said Ira standing and turning toward the Orb. The others followed suit. They all held hands and closed their eyes and Ira touched the Orb.

Chapter 33

"Where are we?" Sam groaned as she awoke. She was confused and disoriented. She assumed that after traveling as many times as they had, that they were no longer going to be knocked out by the energy of the Orb, but here she was on a sandy floor.

"Where are we now?" she asked again.

"You were hit on the head, are you okay?" asked Margaret in a whisper.

"I was hit? By who?" Sam said, also whispering.

"By them" Margaret said pointing.

Sam looked up to find that they were in the company of some strange looking individuals. They were dressed like the wax statues had been in the Museum. They wore long robes and ceremonial garb that looked ancient. They were adorned in jewelry made of animal skulls and bones that seemed to have some tribal significance. These people were clearly desert dwellers. They were short in stature and their skin was browned by the sun. They didn't look like any tribe that Sam was familiar with, and she was as close to an expert on the peoples of the world as anyone could get. She was well versed in the many cultures of the ancient world, but these people were mysterious to her.

Sam and Margaret were being held in a cage of sorts, made of wood and bone that looked flimsy, but proved solid enough. Sam struck the cage and pulled and pushed, but it wouldn't break. She had a very bad feeling about all of this. Hadn't she been imprisoned enough? She was determined to get herself and her friends out.

"Where are the others?" she asked, her head was still a little fuzzy after being unconscious for so long, but it was beginning to clear.

"When we got here, you were almost immediately hit by one of these guys, Jake and I ran off in one direction, and Bernie ran off somewhere else. As for Bernie, I couldn't say, but Jake and I were caught and Rick was pulled off along with you" Margaret explained.

"What about Ira?" said Sam, greatly concerned.

"He...he left us" she said, turning her face toward the ground.

"What do you mean he left us?" said Sam.

"He touched the Orb, he went off alone" said Margaret sighing.

"Shit...he could be anywhere" said Sam.

"I know...but what's more concerning is that we're here" she said.

"What do you think they intend to do with us?" Sam said.

"I can only imagine, but I can tell you that some of these bones are human" she said pointing to the cage.

Sam gasped at the thought that they were in the keep of cannibals. She began to think of ways to escape, but then she remembered that she had the weapon from the prison. She pulled it from her pocket and looked at it as though it was going to tell her exactly how to escape from their cage.

"What are you doing? Put that away before they see" cried Margaret in a loud whisper.

"They don't know it's a weapon or else they would have taken it away before putting us in here" said Sam.

"What's your plan then?" said Margaret.

"I don't know yet, I'll have to think for a while," she answered.

Sam looked through the cage at the encampment where their captors seemed to be bustling about. These people were primitive and gave no sign that they were at all friendly or benevolent.

The camp was large and probably home to fifty or so hostiles. Sam could see several huts that seemed to be the homes of the people that were holding them prisoner. There were men, women and children around so she deduced that they were some kind of tribal family unit. The huts were made of mud and straw and the camp seemed to be generally clumped together around a central fire pit. The pit was large and there were currently several older men sitting around it. They seemed to be praying. The others in the camp were gathering food and placing baskets at the feet of these men that Sam came to realize must be the village elders. She feared that these crude people were preparing to eat her team.

She looked around to try and locate the men, but she couldn't see another cage like the one that held Margaret and herself. The horrifying thought struck her that she might have slept through the consumption of her companions. She quickly dismissed the idea, rationalizing that if these people had eaten her friends, that they wouldn't now be preparing the fire.

"Did you see where they took the boys?" Sam asked.

"No...I haven't seen them since we all ran," she said.

"What about when you and Jake were captured?" asked Sam.

"I was put in here with you, and they took Jake off in that direction...I'm not sure where" she answered.

"Margaret, I'm going to get us out of here, I promise," Sam said, trying to comfort her friend.

"There's more to the village than you can see" said Margaret, "so whatever you're planning, just be careful".

"How much more? Where?" asked Sam.

"We passed it on the way here from the Orb, there's more huts closer to the temple" said Margaret.

"The temple? Is it like our temple?" asked Sam.

"It seems to be, except it's not buried in the ground" answered Margaret.

"Do you think you can lead us back there?" Sam said.

Margaret nodded to say that she could. Sam shifted them to the farthest end of the cage and took a deep breath. She fired the weapon at the opposite end and it exploded leaving the cage tattered and without structure. Sam and Margaret cleared the debris from their path and ran from the cage. The people of the village were scrambling in response to the blast. They seemed to be frightened, but then having no modern technology, Sam had assumed that they would have no idea what was happening. She shouted at Margaret to try and find the guys. She fired another blast toward the frightened group of villagers.

They cowered in response to the crackling explosions. Sam had no idea how this weapon worked or if or when it would run out, so she kept her blasts to a minimum. She had no intention of hurting anyone; she only meant to scare them long enough for her and her teammates to get away. So far, her plan seemed to be working. There were screams and howls of fear from the tribespeople. Sam glared at them in a display of false power. Though she had the weapon, she was not willing to kill them unless they were first going to kill or harm her team. She wished to scare them though, at least into submission for now.

Margaret called out that she had located Jake inside of one of the mud grass huts that encircled the central area. Sam remained outside to keep her hold of fear on the villagers who were running about around the central fire pit, but they were keeping their distance out of fear. Margaret emerged a moment later with Jake in tow. He seemed to be weak and Margaret had to assist him just so that he was able to stand up. Sam was sympathetic at first, but Jake's haggard appearance fueled her already burning anger at once again leading her team to such an unfortunate set of circumstances.

Jake was badly injured and seemed to need great assistance. He was barely conscious and at a glance, it seemed as though he had been severely beaten. His arm appeared to be broken and Sam wasn't sure if it was some kind of dominance ritual or if the cannibals were tenderizing their meat in preparation of their next meal. She had read about ancient rituals that involved beating to death the leader of an opposing tribe after conquest. Perhaps these people had assumed that Jake was their leader as he was clearly the strongest male of the group. They must have beaten him after capturing everyone as a display of victory.

"You two get to the Orb, I'll look for Rick and Bernie" Sam said to them. Margaret nodded and began to help Jake move off in the direction of the temple, which Sam could see now that she was free from the cage and actually standing in the camp. She shot a blast from the weapon again to give cover to the two fleeing slowly from the scene.

Margaret and Jake limped off to the temple that lay about two hundred yards to the side of the primitive camp. Sam's eyes narrowed as she gazed upon the frightened tribe's people. She screamed and shouted at them to tell her where the rest of her team was being held, but it was of no use as they didn't seem to understand English. Why should they, Sam thought, chastising herself for being so dumb. She resolved to look for them herself. She ducked in and out of the grass huts calling out for Rick and Bernie. She kept her powerful weapon trained on the villagers as she conducted her search.

As she circumvented the camp, she noticed another cage on the opposite side from where she and Margaret were being kept. It was similar in construction and size, so she made for it immediately, still shouting her companions' names. She skidded to a dusty halt in front of the cage. Rick was unconscious inside. She wasted no time, she blasted one side open and grabbed him, pulling him across the sandy ground to freedom. She slapped him a few times, but he did not wake. She felt a few warm tears run down her cheeks as the thought struck her that she may lose him. Making a difficult, but quick decision, she was forced to leave him for the moment until she could locate Bernie. She only hoped that her old friend would be in good enough condition to help her carry Rick to the Orb.

Firing off a few more blasts to keep the primitives frightened, Sam searched the few remaining huts. She found Bernie in the last hut in the circle, the irony striking her like a knife. Bernie was tied to a wood pole in the center of the hut with a gag over his mouth.

"Always in the last place you look" she said as she untied her friend.

"That's because you don't keep looking after you find it" said Bernie with half a smile. It seemed that he was uninjured.

"You know, that's a good point, but let's save this discussion for a later date, we gotta get outta here" Sam said, helping the now freed Bernie to his feet.

"Where are the others" he asked as the two bolted from the hut.

"Rick's over here, help me carry him" Sam shouted as she ran for his position. Bernie was close behind her.

They made it to Rick, who was still unconscious. Sam helped Bernie get Rick's limp body onto his broad shoulders. He hoisted him up and they ran from the camp. The villagers were beginning to shout and make threatening gestures as they escaped toward the temple. Sam tried to fire off another shot, but whatever power it was that fueled the weapon had run out leaving them defenseless. Without the fiery blasts to keep them at bay, the angry people of the camp were now giving chase to the three travelers from another dimension. With Rick riding piggyback, Bernie and Samantha fled for their lives.

The temple was not buried here, in this reality, which meant that they were forced to climb up the long flight of stone steps to get to the level where the Orb resided. It seemed to be miles long and was very steep. Margaret and Jake, being injured and sans one shoe were only now reaching the top of the stairs. Sam and Bernie climbed two at a time to attempt to retain their lead on the pack of angry cannibals in pursuit.

By the time they reached the top of the stairs, Sam felt as though her legs were never going to work again. Bernie's breathing was loud and raspy and seemed to describe the pain he was feeling in his lungs. They were both pouring sweat and very tired, but the triumph of having gotten to the top was just enough to keep them going. They disappeared into the temple and made their way as quickly as they were able to the room with the Orb. The villagers were close behind.

Margaret called out to them when she heard their approach. Sam glanced back to see the tribesmen on their tail and she feared they wouldn't make it.

"Go! Touch the Orb! Get outta here!" she cried to Margaret, though she came to regret her words a moment later. The damage, however, was done. Sam rounded the corner into the Orb chamber the very instant that Margaret and Jake disappeared from sight. They vanished only seconds before Sam and Bernie, who was amazingly still carrying Rick, touched the Orb and vanished from sight themselves. The separation was complete and irreversible. Ira was by himself in the vastness of what may be. Margaret and Jake were paired, but still alone somewhere out there, and Sam, Bernie and Rick were all that was left that resembled the original team of six.

Heartbroken and crying, Sam felt nothing as she touched the Orb. There was no fuzzy happy feeling, no pain. There was only her fear and her despair at having been the leader of such a disaster as this. She had been given command of the best team and had led them to failure. She had earned the trust and friendship of some of the most devoted and loyal people and she had allowed them to be tortured, imprisoned, and nearly eaten. Her disappointment, her anguish, her total and complete desolation was as real and as black as the unknown that they now faced. She was lost, both body, and now soul.

Chapter 34

"What are you doing? This is my treasure, you can't be here" said a strange voice from the darkness.

Sam wasn't sure where the voice was coming from, but it had an odd sort of tone to it. It was higher in pitch than a man's voice, but wasn't at all feminine. She looked around in the dark but couldn't see anyone. Her silence only seemed to frustrate the owner of the disembodied words.

"Get outta here, this is my treasure…it's mine and you can't have it!" the voice spoke again.

"We don't want your treasure" said Sam, groggily as she groped in the darkness in an attempt to locate her teammates. Oddly enough, the ground was soft and plush, and Sam came to realize that she was sitting on what felt like a bed. There were pillows and blankets all around her.

She felt a leg beside her. Judging from the girth of the extremity, it belonged to Bernie. She shook him to see if he was alright. Their journey from the last reality to their present one had been more rough and uncomfortable than usual. She thought of Ira's theory about how the Orb reacts to the thoughts of those who touch it, and was forced to conclude that her despair had been reflected back to her as pain when they used it last.

"Bernie" she whispered.

"I said go. This treasure is mine. I won't let you steal it. Get out of here, you can't have it" the voice kept repeating.

Sam now recognized it to be the voice of a child; a young boy. The higher pitch was a sign of his prepubescent state, as was his attitude toward what he called treasure. She assumed he was referring to the Orb. She shook Bernie again and he began to come around.

"Where are we" he asked faintly.

"As if I would know" she answered, annoyed.

"Go away! This is mine! Go away, both of you" cried the boy.

Sam froze for a second. The boy had said 'both' as though there were only two people in the room. This begged the uncomfortable question of Rick's whereabouts. Bernie was definitely carrying him as they touched the Orb, Rick should have been brought here with the two of them. He was unconscious at the time, so he couldn't have gone far. The boy definitely said 'both" though. Frantic and confused, she spread her arms and flailed about the room in an attempt to find him. The room was so dark though, there was absolutely no light.

"I can't see shit in here" she cried in frustration.

"Ooh, you said a cursed word!" the boy exclaimed in horror.

Ignoring him, Sam continued to crawl around and search the black room for her companion.

"Why is it so dark?" said Bernie after a moment.

"What? I don't know, Bernie, do you think you can help me find Rick? We can talk about how lights work later" she barked at him.

"No, I mean, the Orb glows" he said.

Sam froze again. He was right, if they were in a room with the Orb, there should have been some kind of light from the energy of the Orb. The thought hadn't even crossed her mind as she flailed aimlessly in the dark, but Bernie was definitely right.

"So...so where are we?" she said aloud, though it was really more of a thought than an actual question.

"How should I know" Bernie retorted, mocking Sam's earlier quip.

Suddenly the room filled with a blinding light. Sam and Bernie squinted as a door opened on one side of a tiny room that they now occupied. A person had entered their dark little corner and whoever it was stood tall over the three in the darkness. Silhouetted by the contrasting light he towered over the two travelers hunkered on the floor and the child who guarded his treasure so fervently.

Chapter 35

"**A**re you alright?" said Margaret to Jake.

"I think so where are the others?" he said.

"They...they told us to go on without them, remember" she answered sadly.

"Right. And...uh...where are we?" he asked looking around.

"You're in Hospital" she answered.

Jake nodded in acceptance of what she had told him. He did appear to be in a hospital room. He was hooked up to all sorts of machines and IV drip bags. He lay on a bed that was softer and more comfortable than any he had been in for some time. The sound of rain pattered gently on the window. Jake was glad to be inside.

"Are we home?" he asked. His words were careful and his hope was reserved. There had been too many realities, to many cages, to many places that weren't home for him to want to jump to any conclusions.

"I don't think so," she said, casting her head down in disappointment. "We were found in Mali in the temple and everything seemed normal at first, but we aren't home." We were brought here by plane. We are in Chicago. At least we're getting you some medical attention though."

Jake sighed at the news. He was hoping that the familiar nature of the environment would have been a sign that they were finally back, but he was wrong. This was just another alien place, another false home. Familiar had taken on a much broader meaning since their departure from their own reality. Now all it meant was something resembling the home that they had left behind forever.

"It is very similar though" said Margaret.

"What? To our reality you mean?" he said, allowing a tone of excitement to creep into his voice that surprised him.

"I tried to tell them, but with the media and all..." she said. "I couldn't get them to believe me".

Jake was very confused. Who had she tried to tell what? The sheepish and troubled expression on Margaret's face was enough to tell him that he was in for a big surprise in this dimension.

Chapter 36

"You're awake!" said Rick brightly.

"Rick!" exclaimed Bernie and Sam with relief. The person looming over them was less ominous now that they had identified it as their traveling companion. He flipped on the light revealing that they were in a bedroom. There were stacks of toys and cans and sticks all around the corners of the room.

"You scared us, man. Where have you been? Where are we?" said Bernie.

"Tell them not to touch my treasure!" whined the boy.

"Hey, scram kid, we're not going to mess with your treasure, okay" said Rick.

The boy sighed heavily and left the room. Rick beckoned them into the natural sunlight of the next room. Sam and Bernie were confused, but they followed him into the well lit room that adjoined theirs. They appeared to be in a living room. However strange it seemed to the travelers, they were in a place that was more normal than they had been in a long time. Rick sat on a dingy old couch in this strange room in this strange house. The house was antiquated compared to what Sam and the others were used to in their reality. It looked as though it was built in the fifties or the forties. Sam guessed that it hadn't been updated since then.

The walls were covered in an old, ugly floral wallpaper that was peeling down from every seam. The brown glue was left neglected to be revealed on the walls where the paper was missing. The furniture was also outdated and lacking upkeep. The couch that Sam and Rick had seated themselves upon was a dirty shade of crème that had been so ignored for so long that it now had just about every color of stain on it in some place or another. The coffee table that sat between them and the discolored green chair that sat Bernie was bubbled up from years of spills and had several circular stains from glasses that had been placed there with no coaster. There was garbage everywhere and the house reeked like a trash can. Sam thought it looked an awful lot like her college dorm room.

There was a rug covering the hardwood floor that looked as though it used to be some shade of white, but was no more. There were stains covering it and the drapes and just about everything in this strange house. It occurred to Sam that the oddest thing about this place, the thing that preyed most on her mind was that the Orb was absent. Wherever they currently were, they were not near the Orb. Thus her first question to Rick was on that very subject. He seemed to know more than anyone else at the moment so she and Bernie questioned him about everything that he had come to understand about this new reality in which they found themselves.

"Where is the Orb?" said Sam to Rick.

"Oh, it's safe, the kids know not to touch it" said Rick as though his words would be comprehensible by the other two.

"Where is it?" said Sam again.

"It's in the temple, about five miles from here through town," he said.

"I see, so we're in a town?" said Bernie.

"Yes" said Rick "I'm concerned though, because none of the kids have seen Margaret or Jake".

Sam signed. It seemed that there were two stories here that needed reconciling: her's and Bernie's while Rick was out and his while she and Bernie were out. She scratched her head and began where she figured he left off.

"Okay, so we were in that camp with the cannibals" she began.

"Cannibals!" Rick exclaimed, alarmed.

"It's okay, we aren't there anymore" said Bernie in his chipper way.

"Yeah, so that was the last reality, we barely escaped," said Sam.

"You and Sam were hit over the head" Bernie offered helpfully.

"You may not remember much," said Sam.

"I remember arriving in the temple and you were hit. Margaret and Jake ran and Bernie ran. I was trying to get you up and...Ira touched the Orb...That's the last I remember before waking up here" Rick said.

"Well, that's right as far as I know. I came in a cage, you were in a cage too" said Sam.

"Sam broke us all out but you were knocked out so I carried you" said Bernie.

"We touched the Orb and it felt..." said Sam looking for the words to describe the anguish she had experienced.

"It was different...painful...more painful" said Bernie.

Rick was silent for a second. He had no recollection of the cannibals or of the desert camp. He was graciously spared these memories. As well he was spared the uncommonly painful Orb trip that the other two had experienced this time around.

"That must be why you were out for so long," he finally said.

"How long?" said Sam.

"Nearly eighteen hours," Rick responded.

Their reaction was that of great surprise. They had felt the groggy aftereffects, but Sam and Bernie had no idea that they had been out for so long.

"We found you in the hidey hole" said the child who was seated on the filthy carpet in front of them.

"The...hidey hole?" said Sam, raising one eyebrow.

"Yeah, the one we found in the forest" he said as though it was common knowledge that there were hidey holes in the forest.

Sam was clearly confused as was Bernie. They were silent, but looked to Rick for some sort of explanation for this child and his ramblings. Rick was stifling a laugh.

"The temple in the woods" he said smiling "the kids use it for hide and seek".

Sam's face was horrified. The thought that children would use an ancient temple for play was not only frightening for the dangers that such an environment presented, but offensive because of the potential Archeological finds that they might destroy.

"They...kids have been playing in the temple!" she squeaked.

"Not our temple, some other temple though" said Rick.

"I need to speak to their parents!" said Sam raising both brows now going from confusion to panic.

"Good luck," said Rick, shaking his head.

He hadn't told them his side of the story yet, and his was a far more interesting one than a few cannibals.

"There are no parents," he said.

"What!" said Bernie in disbelief. He was sure that Rick was pulling their leg, but his face read complete earnestly.

"You can't have children without parents" said Sam, sure that he was kidding. She was a little perturbed by his flippant attitude as well. It was out of character for Rick to be dismissive of genuine concerns, and yet he was insistent of his outrageous claims.

"They have parents, I assure you, but said caregivers are decidedly...absent" said Rick, squinting his eyes secretively at the other two. Sam sensed his deceptiveness and decided to play along with his mystery.

"So...these parents that are absent...will their offspring meet up with them again in the future?" she said.

"Yes, at least that is what they believe," he said.

"This future meeting of birth givers and those birthed, when does this occur?" said Bernie, following suit.

"Their future rendezvous is thought to occur in or around the age of thirteen" said Rick.

Their eyes turned to the child sitting on the floor. He seemed disinterested in their conversation altogether. He was playing with a toy of some sort and wasn't even paying attention.

"According to the information that I have amassed thus far in my stay here, all the youths in question are between the ages of five and twelve. It would seem as though we are currently located in a kind of maturing grounds wherein the youths are meant to raise themselves in accordance to how generations before them were likewise raised" said Rick.

This manner of speaking was beginning to bother Sam, though she sensed that there was some meaning behind it. The boy on the rug was soon bored and left the room to play outside. Rick spoke again, this time more plainly.

"They get bored if you use what they call fancy talk," he said, plainly.

"I see," said Sam.

"They aren't the only ones" laughed Bernie.

Rick went on to explain in plain English that they were in some kind of colony of children ages five to twelve. There were no adults, no parents, and thankfully, no guards. Of all that he explained of his waking up there and being initiated into this never never land, the most fascinating point was that they were not in Mali.

"One of the kids showed me on an atlas that we are in South America" said Rick.

"Strange, why would they intentionally place the Orb here with all these kids?" said Sam.

"I don't think they did, the kids found a cave that leads to an underground tunnel that leads into a temple. It's their hidey hole and nobody knows about it" said Rick.

"But then, why aren't we in Mali?" said Bernie.

The three of them were at a loss. Ultimately they decided that the Orb must have been moved here at some point in the history of this reality.

"Perhaps not," said Bernie.

"What do you mean?" said Rick.

"I think it's the other way around. Think about the jungle we were in, that was way more likely to be South America than Africa" he said.

"So you think that the Orb was moved at some point in the history of our reality?" said Rick, fascinated.

Sam was also fascinated by the thought, but she was way more concerned by the need to get her team back together than she was in history right now.

"Do you think you can get us back to the Orb from here?" she said to Rick.

"Yeah sure" she said.

"Okay let's go" she said, getting up and heading for the door.

"Right now?" said Bernie.

"Well..." she looked at the two men.

"Sam, don't you think that we should eat and maybe rest up before we head on?" said Rick.

He had a valid point, but Sam was overcome by the need to find the rest of her team. She sat back down on the dirty sofa next to Rick and sighed heavily with discontent.

"Look, we have more to gain by sticking around for a while," said Rick.

"We need food and shelter for a while, we've had it rough" said Bernie.

They were right, but Sam didn't want to admit it at the time. She was so consumed by the distress of the crew being split up and them being in a world of juveniles while the others were god knows where that she couldn't think straight about anything. She sat on the couch and fumed with anguish. Rick sensed her grief and warmly wrapped his arm around her shoulders as he had done in the prison. Bernie noticed their tender moment and rapidly departed from the room under the ruse that he was going to look for food. He was sick of watching the two of them play at flirting. They were so sneaky about it; so sneaky in fact that neither of them was even aware of the other's feelings. They just had these little moments and occasional looks and it was getting on Bernie's nerves.

Chapter 37

Jake lay on his hospital bed staring at the ceiling. He was as lonely here as he had been in that horror dungeon of a prison. His only comfort here was that Margaret was faithfully by his side. She slept softly in a chair next to his bed as the rain fell noisily outside. A passing thought in Jake's mind compared the rain falling against the window to his hopes dropping loudly to the floor with every moment that passed that they were not home. He was drenched in his own misery and in his own memories.

Margaret stirred next to him in the darkness of the hospital room. His dark and treacherous thoughts must have awakened her from her peaceful slumber. She lifted her eyelids drowsily and gazed at him, smiling.

"How can you smile at me?" he whispered with a small tear running down his cheek.

"What? I...I could always smile at you" she said.

She took note of the single tear rolling across his pensive face. She quickly got to her feet and moved herself to the side of his bed to comfort him.

"What's wrong?" she said lovingly.

"I can't do it...I can't bring you home," he said.

"Aww, that's just the pain meds talking" she said smiling and dismissing his words as ramblings.

"No!" he said, grabbing her wrist as she brushed the hair from his face. "I can't give you what you want. I...I just want to make you happy and I can't take you home" he cried.

"Darling...You make me happy no matter where we are" she whispered. Then in an uncharacteristic display of affection, Margaret leaned over and kissed Jake on the forehead. She started to sit up again, but hesitated, as though the kiss on his head was so nice that she needed more. She leaned over and kissed him again, this time on the lips. He lovingly and tenderly kissed her back. As they parted lips, Jake gave Margaret a strange look.

"I don't deserve you," he said.

Overcome by happiness and girlish delight, Margaret began to laugh hysterically. She had never in her forty years been told that she was a prize of a woman. Her laughter grew as she imagined herself a fly on these hospital walls; to see a man as attractive and buff as Jake to tell a dumpy hag like her that she was something special was as comical a scene as any stand up show. To Jake's bewilderment, she laughed harder with each second.

"What's so funny," he said.

"You...You love me" she said between giggles.

"Yeah...I guess I do," he said, still bewildered.

Suddenly Margaret stopped laughing. She stared at him as though he was insane.

"You love me," she said again.

"Yeah, I love you, Margaret," he said.

"I love you Jake" she said, stunned by his honesty and his affection.

They leaned in close and kissed again. He had only one hand free as one was in a cast, but with his one free hand he grabbed her gently and pulled her closer to him. She was so warm and so sweet. He kissed her again and again.

Chapter 38

Bernie entered that tiny kitchen of the house that they found themselves in after landing in this reality. There was an ill repaired stove and an oven with no door. There was a refrigerator, but it was empty from top to bottom. Bernie slammed the door shut loudly. He checked the cupboards only to find that they were almost as empty as the fridge. The only things that they held were spider webs and mold, though. It seemed that there were no edibles in the entire kitchen. He closed each cabinet door more loudly than the previous one. He grunted and kicked the furnishing of the kitchen, finally giving to his anger. He felt claustrophobic suddenly in this antiquated and dilapidated little house. He felt as though the walls were closing in on him and he began to sweat profusely.

He glanced out to the adjoining living room only to see that Sam was crying on Rick's shoulder. He was sick; sick of this journey through the unknown; sick of Rick; sick of having to scrape for food and other necessities. He felt as though he had enough of this and his frustration sent him into a tantrum of anxiety and hatred. He mumbled curses and swears and kicked and punched at anything that happened to be in his way. Luckily all that was there for him to take his anger out on was cabinets and a few empty bread boxes.

He seized one tin bread box and slammed it to the ground and then kicked it clear across the linoleum kitchen floor and out the screen door that led outside from the kitchen of this dirty little abode. He stared at the empty kitchen and at the fresh tear in the screen door. He stared at the living room door and at the empty refrigerator. He could feel the anger and stress welling up inside of him like a volcano that was ready to erupt. He then released a noise that all those present would have described as pure, irate evil in its darkest, black hate.

Sam and Rick came running into the room where Bernie stood fuming with livid breaths of frustration. He stood hunched in the center of the kitchen with his fists clenched and his nostrils flaring. Sam had never seen him in this state and Rick's eyes were wide. It was only a minute ago that they were having a clam, admittedly odd, but serene conversation and now here was their friend billowing the proverbial smoke from his ears.

"Bernie, are you...you okay?" said Sam.

His response was merely a far off stare. There was no acknowledgement that he heard her at all. She cleared her throat and asked again. Again, there was no response but his heavy, irate breathing.

"Bernie...what's up?" said Rick, trying to be supportive.

Bernie looked up at him with a glare that communicated his pure and unrequited hate. It left no room for interpretation. He seemed to snarl as he glared blackly at Rick, who, sensing the hostility, quickly backed down and returned to the living room. Sam remained in the grimy kitchen with Bernie to see if she could fix whatever his disorderly conduct was concerning.

"Bernie, tell me what's going on, because you are kind of starting to scare me" she said honestly.

"There is..." Bernie began, but then seeing Samantha's sweet and worried face, he lightened his mood. He sighed and finished the sentence with the words 'no food' hoping that his hefty size would lend credence to these false words. In truth the rest of the sentence was 'there is no reason that you should fall for this geek when I have been here all along, right before your eyes'. He hadn't the strength to say as much though. Sam was so sweet and so beautiful that he couldn't break her will further than it had been broken. His words; the truth of what he was feeling right now would only serve to hurt her, and Bernie couldn't do that. He blinked rapidly as though blinking would hide the truth that lay in his eyes; the real reason behind his outburst. He searched his mind for something to say to explain the true motive for his actions, but to his surprise, his saving grace came in the form of a child's words.

"They drop food every eight hours," said the little girl who stood in the broken screen of the storm door of the kitchen.

"Hey, what's your name" asked Sam.

"Loretta" said the tiny girl.

Sam smiled and welcomed her inside. The girl was timid, and understandably so given the violent nature of Bernie's temper tantrum. She seemed afraid at first, but eventually she entered and sat with them in the living room.

"What are your names?" she asked in her tiny voice.

"Well, I'm Samantha, and this is Rick and this is Bernie" said Sam.

"I knew a girl named Samantha, but she left last year," said the girl child.

"Left, why?" said Rick.

"She was turning thirteen years," said Loretta.

"Thirteen is when people leave?" said Sam.

"Uh huh" the girl answered with an emphatic nod.

"Is there anyone here like us?" said Sam.

"There's no one here as old as you. How old are you, anyway?" Loretta asked with a sideways look, as though she had uncovered a secret.

"How old do you think we are?" said Rick, smiling.

"Gosh, you look pretty old, I bet you're twenty!" she said.

"Would it surprise you to know that I'm almost forty," said Rick.

"Whoa!" she exclaimed.

"Me too, I'm thirty six" said Sam.

"Wow, that's old!" Loretta said with her eyes wide.

"And Bernie here, he's almost fifty!" said Sam with her eye wide, humoring the child.

"No way! That's...that's half of a hundred" she cried.

This playful teasing did not serve to better Bernie's mood. He was forty eight, but he didn't need it tossed in his face at this particular moment. He already felt shitty enough.

In speaking to the girl they were able to learn more about this reality. The food she spoke of was delivered by plane every eight hours. The kids split it up amongst the entire group and that was how they fed themselves every day. The girl child told them that they usually got boxes of cereal and jugs of juice. She told them ardently that she did not like veggies, but that they too were often in the food deliveries. The entire town would gather and feast on whatever meal they had been given and that was the way of things.

They talked a while longer with the girl. She was barely six and Sam found her extremely cute, whereas Rick seemed to find her company more amusing than anything else. Bernie seemed to despise the child's presence. He wanted to pout but she was too cute to pout around and he resented it terribly. Young Loretta had the type of cherub face that no one could resist. One couldn't help but be nice to her and Bernie was in no mood to be nice. He had a black cloud above his head and he was in no mood for this little angel to clear it away. Loretta, sensing that he was distressed kept looking at him with her puppy dog eyes that just screamed for love and attention. His sympathy was winning out over his anger and eventually he gave in.

With his mood significantly brighter, he joined in asking her questions and talking to her, but on the back burner of his mind he kept warm his red hot anger from before. He could only subdue the hatred; he was unable to rid himself of it, even in the face of this tiny angel. The affection between Rick and Sam was becoming more noticeable every day and it was tearing Bernie apart inside. He had idolized her for so long as his friend and hoped that someday their friendship would grow into something more, but here she was being flirtatious with this nerd from the tech lab. He felt slighted and unloved and unappreciated. All these years he had been by her side and now, as if from nowhere she turned to Rick for support. Sure he was younger and better looking, but he thought that their solid and long-lived friendship would outweigh this geek's new charm.

In truth, Rick's only charm was his respect and admiration for Sam and the person he had come to know as her true self. He was awkward and fumbling most of the time, but his clumsy approach had worked as far as Sam was concerned. Mostly she responded to Rick because he was genuine in his affection for her. Though veiled to the others of their group, he had made no attempt to hide from her his devotion. She had fallen for it only because there was nothing to fall for; it was plain as day that he cared for her. Bernie had for years hidden his true feelings, almost as though he was trying to trick her into a lustful relationship. Rick seemed only to want to treat her. Sam, though unaware of Bernie's romantic feelings, was beginning to be comfortable with her's for Rick.

Chapter 39

Margaret shook Jake awake in his hospital bed. She was still smiling from their admission of love the night before. She had never felt this complete happiness before. She felt as though her face was paralyzed in a permanent grin. She was even more at peace that morning when she saw his eyes open to look at her. He smiled; while he had never been one for getting up early, somehow, waking to her was alright.

"They tell me there's family here to see you" she whispered.

Jake was excited at first, but she then remembered that they were not home, whatever family was there; they were not his. They belonged to a different Jake Baxter, one that had no doubt left his sisters too, but the Baxter sisters that were visiting this hospital were not his. He sighed heavily at the thought that he may never introduce his sisters, his real sisters to the woman he loved.

"I told them not to let the family see us," said Margaret.

Jake looked at her with pleading eyes. She understood them to say that he was hurt by this ongoing episode of being everywhere but home. She agreed, but reiterated to him that they were not home, and that they must try to get there as soon as he was well.

"How do you know we aren't home? I mean can't we just see our families this once, even if we're not home, at least we will have seen our loved ones one last time" he said.

"That wouldn't be fair to them or to us. I know we aren't home, because when we arrived, they told me at the dig site that Sam had died in a cave in weeks ago. I should have left then, but they offered medical attention, and you really need medical attention" she said smiling at him.

"So, we were missing here too, right?" said Jake.

"Yes, everything seems to be right except for Sam dying and a few other minor things" she said.

"So why can't we just..." he began.

"We can't let these families believe that their...that we...that their us's...have come home" she said. Jake knew she was right.

"I just wanted to let my sisters meet the woman I'm in love with" he said, sighing.

"Well you can introduce me to them when we get back" smiled Margaret.

Suddenly Jake's face changed. It seemed to Margaret that he was starring past her at something. She turned to find that despite her explicit orders to the doctors and nurses and other hospital staff, there standing behind them in the doorway to the room was their family.

With no other course of action, they greeted their families and welcomed them inside. The damage was already done. From the hallway of the hospital marched the closest members of the Lishman and Baxter families. They stood there crying at the foot of Jake's bed. Margaret stood and awkwardly introduced her side.

"Uh...Jake this is the *likeness* of my father, Henry Lishman, and my brother Arthur Lishman and my sister Jane Lishman" she said.

"Likeness...you always were weird Margaret. And it's Dubois now, remember" said her sister Jane sticking out her ring finger to show off her diamond.

"Ooh, when did this happen!" exclaimed Margaret, forgetting for a moment that they were not home and that this was not her sister.

"Three years ago...you were there, dear" said Jane, worried.

Margaret looked at Jake as though to say that it was going to be very difficult when that had to tell them the truth. Jake wasn't looking back at her though, he was staring at his family. Margaret was quiet for a moment to allow him to speak.

"Uh, Margaret these are my two sisters...and my parents" he said in a wavering, shaky voice.

"Hello, I'm Bruce and this is my wife Alison, we're Jake's parents. These are our daughters Erin Baxter and Erica Baxter" said the man who looked like Jake's Father.

"Margaret Lishman" she said, kindly, though she was very concerned about the look on Jake's face.

"My parents are dead" Jake blurted out suddenly.

"Oh, Jake!" cried his mother, covering her mouth in shock.

"What an awful thing" said Jane.

"You don't understand, we aren't your family, we come from another dimension and…" Jake said looking at Margaret to explain the rest.

"You see, we found this device that transports us from one reality to another and we've been trying to get back to our reality. This is not our reality. My sister Jane is not married and Jake's parents are no longer living in our reality" said Margaret.

The faces of their false family members read shock and dismay. They know that the two had been checked out for any brain injury, but yet their claim was absurd. They couldn't and wouldn't believe such a thing, especially when their own Jake and Margaret had gone missing in the same manner as those that stood before them. As far as the families were concerned, they had their loved ones back.

"Alison, get the doctor," said Bruce Baxter.

"I'll go" said Jane to Jake's crying and hysterical mother.

"Wait, she's telling you the truth, there's nothing wrong with us" said Jake, but Jane was already heading out and down the hall.

"We are not your family. We look like them, but they are out there somewhere, just like our real family, our reality is out there somewhere" protested Margaret.

The travelers were unable to convince their look-alike families that what they said was the truth. There was no doctor that would be able to verify their claim. They were in every way what these people wanted; they were Jake Baxter and Margaret Lishman. The only thing that the doctor would be able to back them up on was that they had suffered no head injuries. This at least would support their incredible claim a little. It was probable that everyone would assume that they were suffering from post traumatic stress syndrome or perhaps some other mental illness. This was going to be a difficult scenario to get out of.

Chapter 40

S am and Rick marched through the jungle with Bernie in tow. They followed their ten year old guide to the place where he claimed to have found the cave that led to an old temple. They had just eaten a meal that was airdropped in a few hours ago and the hike was one not easily made on a full stomach. They were all too happy to have a full stomach though after being so empty for so long. The food that was dropped was more than enough for the hundreds of kids that roamed freely about the town.

Sam was still a little fuzzy on the details of the situation, but it had been explained to them by one of the older kids. He had told them that in their society, one was taken here at the age of five to learn to be self sufficient. Many parents in their society brought their kids here. They learned to form alliances and when to trust, they learned to care for one another and they learned to sacrifice. They learned many of the lessons of life here in this harsh environment. Then, on their thirteenth birthday, they were taken back to their families, presumably, better people for having been there.

It sounded like a harsh and unfeeling society to Sam, but then in her reality, there were far too many spoiled children that grew into rotten adults. Steve Philpot was a prime example. Here, the kids were given food and clothing to survive and occasionally toys that they learned to share amongst each other. The boy who had shouted at them had been punished by the rest for hiding toys and cans of food in the bedroom where Rick had stashed them to begin with. His so-called treasure had been divided up for the rest of the children. His punishment was a spanking, administered by each of the other children in their community. According to Hunter, their ten year old guide, there were hundreds of communities around and each of them had their own particular set of rules.

He stopped in front of the hidey hole as it was so named by the children and waved them inside. Sam ducked her head and crawled inside the tunnel made of dirt and tree roots and rocks followed by Rick and then Bernie. She crawled along for a few yards before reaching a place in the tunnel where the dirt turned to stones. It appeared as though the jungle had opened a hole in the side of some ancient temple that was completely covered by the vegetation of the South American rainforest. She hoisted her trim body through the hole.

"It's a little tight up here, but it opens up after that" she called out to the others.

Once through the hole, she stood up to see that she was in a chamber of the hidden temple. It was pretty dark, but there were vines and roots that had grown through the walls in places and that served to provide a little light. The temple was damp and smelled of mildew and soil. Now that she was standing here, Sam could see why these kids thought this place was so cool. This was just the sort of place that she would have tried to explore as a child. A grin formed on her lips as she took in the scenery of the place that she now found herself.

"Neat isn't it?" said Rick.

"Yeah, this is totally awesome" said Sam emphatically smiling.

Rick loved to see her smile like this and he was once again overcome by the urge to kiss her. Once again his tender moment with Samantha was dashed away by Bernie.

"Hey guys...I'm stuck," he cried.

They turned to find that he was lodged in the hole in the wall. His shirt seemed to be stuck on some of the stone that made the outer wall of the temple and he was struggling to free himself of the hole. Sam crawled in to try and dislodge her pal from the tunnel. After a short period of fighting with it, they were finally able to free him and help him into the temple. Bernie took a short look around and commented on how musty it was.

"I know isn't it great," said Sam.

"Great? No it's filthy and wet and stinky" Bernie said.

"Yeah, Bern, that's what's great about it...its ancient" grinned Sam.

Bernie rolled his eyes at her childlike fascination of all things old and icky. They looked around for a moment longer before heading through the halls to find the Orb. Rick led the way. He had come this way when the kids found them at the Orb. He and a few of the children had pulled the others out of the temple and carried them to the nearby town. He had placed their unconscious bodies in the bedroom of one of the houses which was where they awoke eighteen hours later. Having been through here a few times, he pretty much knew where he was going, but it was dimly lit and rather troublesome to navigate. Finally the three of them made it to the Orb chamber.

The temple looked very much like the one in Mali, though it was hard to tell because of the poor lighting and the fact that neither temple had much of anything inside. The similarities were in the labyrinth of the halls and rooms and in the barren aspect of both temples. Sam commented that there were no statues or treasure and asked Rick if he thought that the kids might have taken stuff out of the temple. He answered that the children were afraid of the temple since the disappearance of a few children.

"They likely touched the Orb and disappeared" said Rick sadly "as a result, very few of the kids actually come in here, and they're too afraid to touch anything".

In that moment Sam realized how terrifying it must be for those children who don't know where they are or how to get back. She had never realized that her biggest fear was jumping from dimension to alternate dimension with no one by her side, but in that moment her fears came rushing at her with terrifying force. She had always been afraid of heights and getting mugged, but those were common and realistic fears. Ever since this whole escapade began, she had been terrified of only one thing, and that was having to journey through these realities alone. The thought that there were children out there alone and frightened was too much for her to want to think about.

"We have to touch it" said Sam suddenly.

Rick and Bernie were quiet for a moment as they stared at the Orb in front of them. The dim glow illuminated their pensive, thoughtful faces and made them look almost ghostly.

"We have team members out there alone; there are children out there alone" Sam pleaded.

"You're right" nodded Rick "if we can at least find them, then we'll be better off than we are".

"Are you insane? We should stay here where we are safe and maybe if we get lucky, they'll get home or somewhere safe too" said Bernie.

"I don't even see that as an option, Bernie. The way I see it, we have to keep trying" said Rick.

"Sam, c'mon this is crazy!" said Bernie.

"I'm with Rick on this one" she said.

"Of course you are…You two have become the Orb crusaders on your fucking holy mission to get home and reunite all those lost or some shit" Bernie shouted angrily.

"What's wrong with wanting to get home?" she barked back at him.

"Well let's see, there's the fact that we've lost more than half of our team. It's near impossible to get back anyway, and even if we do we'll be coming home to Yoshido industries landing on our heads and trying to take the Orb" Bernie shouted back at her.

It was a moment later that he realized his big mistake. He could see the shocked and angry faces of his two companions glaring back at him. In the faint light of the Orb's glow they looked almost like demons as they stared at him.

"Yoshido huh, is that who was in the helicopters?" said Sam.

"I…" Bernie stuttered and spat, but couldn't come up with a good lie to excuse his transgression.

"You fuck! You sold us out to Yoshido! How could you do that" screamed Samantha.

"Who is Yoshido?" said Rick.

"They're a Japanese company, major competitors with PhilTech. They offered me a hundred thousand to tell them what I know" said Bernie.

"That was you who met the black hummer that night" said Sam gasping.

"I didn't know anyone saw us, look I just wanted to make a little money okay" said Bernie.

"There is no excuse for this. Jesus, I thought you were my friend" said Sam, hurt by his betrayal.

"That's all I ever was to you was a friend. Do you know that I've been in love with you for years" he shouted back at her.

"And this is how you tell me...Don't fucking change the subject, you betrayed us" she yelled.

"You betrayed me. I have been nothing but loving to you all this time and you ignored it. Then geek here comes on the scene and all the sudden you're swept off your feet" he shouted.

"I never felt that way about you Bernie and you know it. For you to blame this on me is outrageous. The only thing you love is money" said Sam.

"Well it's warmer than you, Sam" he hissed at her.

Sam was silent after his insult. She was truly hurt by his words. Without a word she left the Orb room and crawled back through the tunnel. Rick was alone with Bernie in the temple. He watched as Bernie stood there eating the misery of his own doing.

"You think I'm a shit don't you" said Bernie after a moment.

Rick was silent. He had thought of Bernie as a friend and a good man, but he was beginning to question his judge of character.

"I am you know...I am a shit" said Bernie.

Rick chuckled a little. He had not expected Bernie to say that and though the moment was a serious one, he chuckled just the same.

"You can still make it right with Sam though" Rick said.

"She'll never forgive me for selling her out. She'll never forgive me for loving her either" he said.

"Maybe...Maybe you could start by apologizing to her though" said Rick, and with that he left the temple as well.

Bernie stood in the glow of the Orb for another moment. He thought about how awful he had been. All he wanted was for Sam to forgive him so that he could feel better about himself. She was his friend and if she forgave him, well that would at least be a start. He walked out of the Orb chamber and into the hall. He followed the long winding maze back to the room where they entered. When he arrived, he found Sam and Rick frantically moving the vines and roots that held the crumbling stone in place.

"What are you doing, you're gonna block us in," he said alarmed.

"That's kinda the idea" said Rick as he yanked a root. Several stones came crashing down with a rumbling noise that resulted in a dusty heap of rock that blocked them in.

"Let's get to the Orb" shouted Sam.

"What's going on," said Bernie.

"There's about a thousand kindergartners out there with sticks and rocks who think that we're demons who eat children" said Rick.

"Okay..." said Bernie.

"They said that we're responsible for the missing kids and they aren't happy about" said Sam, grabbing Bernie by the arm and pulling him through the halls.

"Let's get the hell out of this creepy place" yelled Rick.

They could hear the stones being moved from the hole in the side of the temple wall. They ran through to the Orb room. Once there they quickly touched the Orb and hoped for the best.

Chapter 41

J ake and Margaret had been cleared to leave the hospital. Their counterpart families had brought them fresh clothes and had taken them to their hotel for the night. The next day was set for the memorial service for the rest of the team that was lost and for Sam, who had died in this reality. After a sleepless night, they were made to attend the service of their friends who were, as far as they hoped, actually still alive.

The two found each other that day in the funeral parlor. They stood in the back of the large room and looked over all the people that were there to mourn the passing of people who had not yet passed. Maso's family had given their respects to Margaret personally. It was very upsetting t them when she told them that he was probably still alive. Jake had to restrain her as she pleaded with everyone, trying to tell them that their loved ones were still out there somewhere.

No one wanted to listen to what they assumed were the ravings of a mind preyed upon by the symptoms of post traumatic stress syndrome. They only patted her on the shoulder and said things like "hang in there" and "you've been through so much". These sentiments of pity only angered Margaret further.

Jake was doing his best to control and console her, but he too was becoming frustrated at the fact that no one wanted to believe them. They stood on the green carpet of the large room, defeated and oppressed by their own relatives. The chairs were filled with people who were there to pay their respects. Across the room from them was a raised up section of the floor where Sam's casket rested covered in flowers. Next to her coffin was a table that was covered with photos and notes and memories of Rick and Bernie and Maso and Ira. On the other side of Sam's casket was a large stand-up picture of her and a pedestal that held the Orb. Steve Philpot had lent it to them for the funeral and the display was truly beautiful.

Margaret's plans were not to mourn, however. She and Jake were going to touch the Orb and leave this place before they got stuck in therapy for the rest of their lives, which was likely to happen if they stayed. They waited for everyone to pay their respects and were now inching their way around the hall to be closer to the Orb. A minister was saying some lovely words about the team and their friendship with each other.

"These were devoted people" he said "and none more so than the leader of these talented folks, Samantha Byrne. She was so determined, such a leader..."

"You have no idea," said Margaret out loud.

She was given a few dirty looks by the crowd, but the minister continued. It seemed that her behavior was tolerated only because of their incredible return after so long. The sympathy card was over played though and the patience of the patrons was running thin.

"...and they shall be sorely missed" the minister finished a while later.

Steve Philpot took over from there. He walked to the podium and began speaking about his wonderful team who were so loyal and how his own son gave his life for the project. This was very troubling to Jake and Margaret and finally they had had enough of his prattle.

Margaret and Jake stormed up onto the stage where Steve was speaking and crying his crocodile tears. She shoved him out of the way while Jake gave a look of warning to those in the crowd who were beginning to stand up. He wasn't about to let them stop Margaret from speaking her peace. She stood behind the podium and glared out at the group in front of her.

"This man is full of lies" she began, but before she could continue, there was a great light from the Orb.

Everyone's attention was on the glowing sphere as it spun and hovered above its pedestal. Margaret and Jake were shocked.

"What's happening?" he said.

"I…I don't…" she began, but before she could finish her sentence, the explanation appeared before them.

From the Orb's aura of light there appeared several people. It was the missing team; a missing team. There before the baffled crowd stood Ira and Maso and Bernie and Rick and another Jake and Margaret.

"What the hell is going on here" shouted Steve Philpot.

"We're back!" cried Bernie.

"Holy shit, there's two of me" cried the other Jake.

"Um…are you mother and father still living?" asked the Jake at the podium.

"Yeah, in fact they're right there" he answered pointing.

"They belong here" said Margaret in awe.

There was an awkward moment where the two parties looked at each other. Both teams knew that it was possible, but it was still shocking to see. The attendees of the memorial service were stunned and confused. Their heads looked back and forth between the two sets of travelers before them.

"Should we leave?" asked Jake in a whisper.

"Yeah, this is too funky" answered Margaret.

"Do you know how you managed to get here?" said Jake.

"We touched the sphere" said the other Jake.

"No…Was it luck that you got back or did you figure out how to control the Orb?" said Margaret.

"Oh…it was luck I guess," said the Rick of the other team.

"We don't know how it happened but we…We've seen some things" said the other Bernie.

"Us as well," said Margaret.

"They don't know anything that can help us, let's leave" said Jake.

"Good idea" agreed Margaret.

"Thank you everyone, goodbye" Jake said as he grabbed Margaret's wrist and touched the Orb. And just like that, they were blinked out of sight.

It was difficult to think that there could be hundreds or thousands or even billions of realities out there that were so similar to theirs. How many teams were missing? How many Jakes and Sams were lost out there in the far reaches of the unknown? Would the team ever get back as that one had? Moreover, was that really the team that belonged to that reality, or where they, as Jake and Margaret had been, in a reality that was very similar, but not the same? There was no way to know. There was so much that was unknowable to these travelers. Margaret was beginning to understand why the texts had spoken of this as that which is known only to the gods. She was one of the smartest people in the world, and she still couldn't fully comprehend the magnitude of what they were involved in. She felt very much like the meager mortal that she was.

Part Three

Reunion

Ira was standing alone in a darkened room. His face was twisted in sorrow over abandoning his friends. He began to cry softly. He had hardly thought it was possible for him to make even more of an ass out of himself, but yet here he was safe and sound at the expense of his team. He had gone from spy to deserter. For the first time in his life he felt like his father's son. He had always striven to be like the great Steve Philpot, but now that he was, he resented it deeply. He thought over what could have possibly made him act that way. Sure he was afraid after those primitives hit Samantha, but it wasn't just the situation that made him abandon his friends. Perhaps it was the way he was raised or the person he was raised by. Perhaps it was genetic. All he knew was that his father was a horrible man who cared for nothing and no one. This attitude had made Steve Philpot a rich man, but Ira was not his father, and he cared deeply for his companions. Why then had he touched the Orb and left them alone.

He was more disturbed by his own actions than by the situation in which he now found himself. He was alone in an unknown reality in a dark room. There was no one around, and very little light. The only light seemed to be the faint glow of the Orb. There was a dim glow coming from above as well. It seemed to grow brighter as he stood in the empty room. He became aware of this light that was falling like snow from above his head. It was only then that he actually looked up.

He gasped as he took in the amazing sight that hovered far above his head. It was beautiful and strange and mysterious. As he gazed upon this wondrous and breathtaking sight he became aware that he was not alone in this room as he had assumed himself to be.

"Hello, Ira" said a voice that was somewhat familiar.

"Hello" Ira called back, but he had not seen the owner of the voice in the dark room.

"Lovely isn't it" said the voice.

"It's beautiful," whispered Ira.

"You should sleep, you look tired" said the voice.

"I...I am rather sleepy..." said Ira, who was falling into a sort of trance. He could feel himself falling asleep as he spoke the words. This was so strange, and yet he felt as though it was okay. He felt nice, really. He was warm and happy and peaceful. There was a sort of tingly feeling that crawled all over his body and it made him feel such pleasure. This feeling, it seemed so familiar, like crawling into a freshly made bed that's warm and soft. He drifted off into a beautiful, pleasant sleep.

Chapter 43

Weary and disheartened they sat in the room where the orb had deposited them this time. It was dark and warm here. They were alone in this room and had no clue as to their whereabouts. Their spirits were low, but they were hopeful in spite of all that had happened to them.

"I'm so tired of this," said Sam.

"We get held hostage by our friends, trapped in the never ending line, sent to a hellish prison, stuck in a jungle, nearly eaten by cannibals, then we end up in a world where children attack us" said Bernie.

"What's next!" cried Rick, laughing.

"Do you at least forgive me?" said Bernie sheepishly.

"Of course I do. You're still in the dog house, but we're friends, and all we have is each other" said Sam.

"Where do you suppose we are?" said Rick.

The three stood in a circle around the Orb. They were very tired and really didn't have the energy to go groping around in the dark in search of a door. Wherever they were, it was at least safe for now. They looked around as they became aware of a light from above. It was faint but it was enough to get their attention.

They stared up at an enormous Orb floating above them. Suddenly they found that Ira was standing next to them gazing up at the Orb as well. They were so shocked, but somehow they couldn't react with anything but complacency and acceptance. They felt so calm as they stood in the falling petals of light.

Margaret and Jake also appeared from the Orb and they too were overcome by the beauty of the giant shining Orb above them. No one spoke; they only stared and took in the magnitude on this Orb hovering in the darkness over their heads. Here was an enormous ball of brilliant shining energy that dropped like cherry blossoms around them and nobody could say anything. In truth there were no words that could accurately describe the gorgeous sight that lay before them.

"You have seen so many things, been so many places" said a voice.

The reunited team wanted to speak, but they were stuck in such a complete state of comfort that they were unable to articulate words at all.

"You wish now to return home, but first allow me to explain some things to you my friends" said the voice that the team now recognized to be that of Francois. They couldn't see him, but they could all hear him so clearly. It was as though he was standing very close to them, but he was not. His voice wasn't being amplified; it was almost as though he was speaking from inside their heads.

"Margaret, may I say that I'm glad to see that you have received a replacement pair of shoes" said Francois.

"The Orb you have been using belongs to us. We never intended it to be used by Humans. It was my intention to retrieve it before you found it in the temple. Rick you are thinking that we are Aliens. You would not be correct. I am human and yes Sam I am a telepath. My race is what we call Homo Sapiens Primus. Bernie, your Latin is rusty, old man...it's actually the first ones of wisdom. We have used these Orbs for centuries to study and learn from other places and times. We are far older and wiser than your species, though we both have evolved on Earth. We have complete control over the Orbs. You are correct Ira, we use our minds to operate the Orbs. Perhaps when your species is older, we may live harmoniously, but until then, we shall remain unknown to the Human race."

"I shall return you now" Francois said out loud this time.

The team was released from their trance and they could now see the man standing before them. They were thoroughly shocked by all that they had been told, but somehow they knew it to be true. It was as though they had gained complete understanding suddenly. The feeling of being in the know was quite empowering, but they still had so many questions, so many things to ask Francois about. They began to pelt him with questions about his race and about the Orb, but he only grinned a toothy smile and stared back at them.

They would have thought it very odd except that they suddenly felt very good. That warm fuzzy feeling crept over them and their eyes rolled back in their heads. They felt tingly all over. Slowly the feeling faded and they came to realize that they were back in the temple.

Chapter 44

"Wait...I had more questions!" shouted Ira.

"We're back! We're back!" hooted Jake grabbing Margaret and spinning her around joyfully and kissing her.

"Hey guys! Long time no see!" said a familiar voice.

"Maso!" they cried in unison.

"Where have you been?" asked Margaret.

They hugged their long lost friend and each other repeatedly. They were elated to be back.

"So, Maso, what happened to you?" said Sam.

"I could ask you the same thing" he said taking note of their tattered and bloody and muddy clothes.

"We...We ran into some trouble," said Rick.

"Where did you end up?" Bernie asked.

"I was sent through time to the future! There were flying cars and aliens! It was amazing!" he said.

"The future?" asked Sam.

"Yeah, it was really cool for a while, but then I decided to come home. I just got back a few minutes ago" said Maso

"But...the orb sends you to alternate realities," said Rick.

"Oh, well I guess that makes sense too" he said.

"So...wait...you only went to one reality before you got back here?" said Ira.

"Yeah..." he said.

"You always had all the luck," said Margaret.

"Why...where did you go?" he asked.

"We don't wanna talk about it," said Sam.

"Okay...but seriously...could you guys maybe shower or something?" he said to the four who were dirty and hadn't changed clothes.

They laughed and made their way through the tunnels and out of the temple. They left the secret room. It was dark and empty now without the Orb, which Francois had presumably removed. The heat from the African sun struck them as they walked out of the temple into the day. They climbed the ladders of the dig site to the top.

There didn't seem to be anyone around. There were no helicopters, no diggers, no sign of anyone. The dark thought crossed their minds that they might have been dropped into yet another reality that wasn't their own. As they walked through the camp they saw that everyone was there, after all. Their entire crew seemed to be eating lunch in the mess hall. The six proudly strutted into the huge tent and excitedly announced that they were back.

"Great, can we eat please?" said Pete.

"I thought you'd be happy to see us after so long," said Sam.

"It's been like...five minutes" said Pete.

"Whoa, what happened to your clothes?" said Karissa.

"Jesus! Are you okay!" said Darrius taking notice of Sam's filthy sweat soaked shirt.

"Five minutes?" was all she was able to say.

The team looked at each other with confusion. They didn't want to, but they had to believe that they had not in fact returned home.

"They have no idea," said Francois from behind them.

The team turned suddenly. They stared at him for a moment before he explained what was happening.

"It's as if you never touched the Orb," he said.

"And what about the helicopters?" asked Bernie.

"Never happened" said Francois.

"How is this possible?" asked Sam.

"Did you think that the Orb that you have been using was the only one we have?" he said grinning.

They were stunned by his words.

"What the hell are you guys talking about!" said Pete.

"It's...uh...A joke, a practical joke...never mind" said Sam.

The people in the mess hall all starred with raised eyebrows at the seven travelers. They excused themselves and headed off to the showers. They bathed thoroughly and changed their clothes.

Chapter 45

Rick crossed over the sand to Sam's trailer. He knocked and was let in by Karissa and Brad. He greeted them and inquired as to Sam's whereabouts. They motioned at the office. He opened the door and stepped inside.

"Rick," she said, a little startled by his sudden entry.

"Sorry, I didn't mean to startle you," he said.

"It's okay, what's up?" she said.

"I...I wanted to say..." he stuttered.

Seeing that he was having trouble saying whatever was on his mind, Sam crossed the room to him.

"What is it?" she said.

He stared at her face for a moment. Then with no prelude whatsoever he kissed her. It was a kiss that was long and passionate and unrestrained. He was so relieved and so happy to have finally been able to do what he had wanted to do for so long. He was completely unbridled as he caressed her face and arms. It was as though he had exploded with passion. When the kiss ended he smiled at her.

"I wanted to tell you that I love you," he said.

Sam gazed back at him. She was so surprised by his ardor that she was rendered speechless for a moment. She wanted to tell him she felt the same way; she wanted to, but was too caught up by the heat of the moment. Not being able to find the words, she simply kissed him again.

Chapter 46

"Whoa! You gotta come check this out!" cried Karissa.

"Whatcha got?" said Sam.

"It's some kind of sphere," she answered.

Sam jerked her head around to see that Karissa was holding a golf ball sized object in her hand. She sighed with relief. It was far too small to be an Orb. It was covered with dirt and mud and Sam assumed that it must just be some trinket of the civilization that built this place.

"Faked you out didn't she" laughed Rick who was digging in the dirt next to Sam.

"She had me worried for a second" Sam laughed.

"Seriously you gotta see this" said Karissa handing the object to Sam.

Sam took it and held it for a moment. As it rested in her hand she became aware that the sphere was glowing. It looked like a tiny version of the Orb.

"Rick!" she shouted.

He looked up to see her troubled face as she held the tiny glowing Orb in her hand. Suddenly he became very worried. He lunged toward her, knocking the thing out of her hand. It rolled across the dirt of the bottom level of the temple.

"What the hell is wrong with you two?" asked Karissa bending down to pick up the small sphere.

"Don't touch it!" cried Sam and Rick at nearly the same time.

"Why...What's wrong?" she asked.

"We...we don't know what it does," said Rick wide eyed.

About that time Bernie and Ira entered the chamber on the lowest level of the temple. Seeing the tiny Orb they both screamed.

"Kill it! Kill it!" shouted Ira.

Karissa snatched up the Orb while Bernie tried to stomp it with his boot.

"What the hell is wrong with everyone, this is an incredible find" she scolded them.

"Put it down please" cried Ira.

"No! I'm taking it to the lab" she said.

They jumped up and followed her through the jungle to the lab building. This new dig site was pretty amazing. State of the art thanks to the incredible amount of gold that had mysteriously appeared in the temple in Mali. Sam sort of assumed that Francois had something to do with that. Steve Philpot had been quite pleased. He was expecting a new piece of technology, but he got gold, which was just as good to him. Their share had been more than enough to set up this current dig in South America.

Sam was thrilled to find that there was a temple in their reality that matched the one that the children had called their hidey hole. So far, they had uncovered many interesting finds. The layout of the temple was the same as the one in Mali and in ancient Mesopotamia. This was exciting stuff.

She had been elated for the past several weeks of this dig, but now she was frightened. Was this tiny thing an Orb? She was not about to let Karissa be whisked off to another reality. The four ran after her shouting and screaming for her to drop it.

"You people are crazy!" Karissa said once inside the lab building.

"She hasn't disappeared yet, maybe it's not an Orb" said Bernie.

"Look at it...I mean it looks just like it," said Ira.

"Looks like what!" cried Karissa.

The four were speechless. There was nothing to say that she would believe. They urged her to put it down, but she was fascinated by it. She finally placed it on the lab table and returned with the others to the temple.

"That was a close call" said Sam.

"I can't wait to tell Jake and Margaret about this, though," said Rick.

"How is she anyway?" asked Bernie.

"She's doing well, it was a difficult one because of her age, but they both came out fine" said Sam.

"What were they?" asked Karissa.

"One boy, one girl" answered Sam.

"Imagine having twins and at the age of forty-too" said Karissa.

"Forty is still young," said Bernie.

"I bet Jake is pleased," said Rick.

"Oh, I've never seen him so happy," said Sam.

Suddenly there was yelling from the temple. Sam and her team ran for the site where they were met by several of the local diggers. They were saying something about a magical glow coming from one of the chambers in the temple. They seemed to be terrified. The five of them entered to find that there was a pedestal in the center of one of the rooms. It was giving off a strange light that reminded them of the giant Orb, but it was coming from the pedestal. This pedestal looked just like the one that the Mali Orb had hovered above, but it had no Orb atop it.

The glowing light seemed to be almost solid and it was growing toward them. Karissa's face was paralyzed in a picture of awe and wonder. She reached out her hand and touched the light. It was as though the light was water. It was tangible, but she could move her hand right through it. Suddenly, in a silent and horrifying moment, she disappeared before their very eyes. In a breath she was gone.

Don't miss out!

Visit the website below and you can sign up to receive emails whenever Emily Vaughn publishes a new book. There's no charge and no obligation.

https://books2read.com/r/B-A-WNFN-VBULB

BOOKS 2 READ

Connecting independent readers to independent writers.

www.ingramcontent.com/pod-product-compliance
Lightning Source LLC
Chambersburg PA
CBHW051427130726
47987CB00005B/1951